GABRIELLE MARIE KOZAK

Renée

reborn

For the real-life Dusty and Casey. God bless you.

"Once you're here, you're here to stay."

— Cassandra Sicario

Contents

One

❧

Downtown Manhattan, New York, 1956

"Have a good day, Trisha!"

"See you, Dad!" The sixteen-year-old tripped down the front steps gaily, closing the door carefully behind her.

Her father watched her through the window, smiling proudly.

As the girl's neatly cut golden hair disappeared down the street on her way to school, Florian Lee let the window curtains fall back silently. He stepped away from the window, sipping his cup of coffee as he glanced down at a folder that lay on the table.

He frowned, and then set his coffee down swiftly, snatching up the folder and opening it.

Florian's face fell as he was confronted with his daughter's school papers. He dropped the folder like hot coal, rushing back over to the front door.

Throwing it open, he shouted his daughter's name.

"Trisha!"

There was no answer. But of course there wasn't—Trisha would already be well on her way to school.

Snapping his fingers, Florian gave himself a quick glance in a mirror that hung conveniently close to the front door, brushed an invisible speck or two of something off his jacket, and left the house, running in the direction Trisha had taken.

He hadn't gotten down the front steps when he was accosted by a hooded young woman who glanced hard at him and then blocked his way.

Startled, Florian glanced back at her, his blue eyes confused.

"Mr. Florian Lee?" the girl asked him softly, pushing back her hood.

Now he could see her—short red hair, dark blue eyes that seemed almost black, and a quietly cold atmosphere about her. About eighteen, she was dressed all in black, a hoodie extending far over her forehead.

He glanced over her before nodding. "Well, that's my name. May I help you?"

"I have a message to deliver," the young woman confided, glancing both ways almost cautiously. "In private."

"One moment—I have to—" Florian began, glancing back towards the street.

He stopped short when his anonymous visitor shook her head.

"It'll be only a few seconds," she assured him, continuing to block his path. "And it's urgent."

Her voice was quiet and clear, but Florian's eyes narrowed.

Then he retreated up the steps to the house. "Fine. But make it quick."

He opened the door and held it open for her. He didn't miss the look she shot at him as she stepped past him and into the hallway.

Closing the door softly, Florian stood against it and turned to face her. "Now, miss, what brings you here?"

Her dark eyes glinted steel briefly. "If you're Florian Lee, the famous detective, then you've heard of Nelson Coligny, current leader of the Mafia in Manhattan, am I correct?"

Florian's thoughts changed in an instant, but not a muscle of his face moved.

Watching the girl's eyes carefully, as if he could read her next motions in them, he nodded wordlessly.

The girl smiled slightly, then looked down momentarily. "Well, I have a message for you—from him."

Her hands were hidden in the folds of her dark clothing, but now one emerged partway.

"Fire away," Florian told her coolly.

The atmosphere in the hallway changed.

She looked up, and his blue eyes met her dark ones. Florian reached quite deliberately for the place on his belt where his gun could be found.

The girl's hand moved faster than lightning, and before Florian could pull arms or even call out for help, the assassin's knife was in his throat. He stared at her unbelievingly as his hands flew up—and then slowly he toppled over.

Kneeling at his side, the girl retrieved her knife casually, wiping it meticulously on the detective's clothes.

Her smile became grim and businesslike as she leaned down and whispered into his ears, even as his eyes clouded over.

"The message is: The shrimp that falls asleep gets carried away by the current. Sweet dreams, Detective Lee," she whispered; and closed his eyes.

There was no answer, and there never would be, once Nelson Coligny's best assassin carried out her work. But she hadn't finished.

She straightened after patting down the detective's pockets. They were empty.

The assassin stood up, slipping her knife back into her belt with gloved hands after notching it with another. There were already plenty of notches on the handles of all her knives.

"It's here *somewhere*," she muttered to herself, glancing around the hallway.

There was obviously nothing there, and she wandered into the kitchen, not unaware of the oppressively quiet stillness that hung over her surroundings. Now she was the only one alive in the place, and the house seemed to sense it.

Finally she espied the folder that Florian had left on the table—the folder Trisha had accidentally left behind when she took her father's folder instead.

The assassin's eyes brightened as she picked up the folder, but the gleam vanished from her eyes when she realized it contained only school papers.

Sighing, she replaced the folder carefully on the table and went to search the rest of the house.

* * *

A teenage boy paced up and down in front of the Lee residence, his hands in his pockets and his eyes glued to his shoes.

Occasionally he glanced up at the house, but every time he shook his head, disappointed. He seemed to be waiting for someone, even if his constant turning around made it obvious that he didn't know what direction that someone would be coming from.

But a few minutes later, when the front door of the Lee home opened silently and a young woman a couple of years older than he was stepped out, the boy stopped pacing and stared up at her with something like irritation coming over his face. It was doubtful that he'd expected her to be leaving *that* house.

She saw him as well, and hopped lightly down the steps after closing the door carefully behind her. The two fell into step with each other, heading down the street.

The girl's red hair shone in the early morning sunlight—that is, until she pulled her hood back up over it.

The boy glanced up at her, his face anxious. His eyes narrowed as they lit on a small crimson splash on his older sister's sleeve.

"Casey—"

"Shh," she warned, not meeting his gaze. "Dusty, what's up?"

"Casey," he repeated, more quietly this time but more urgently as well. "You've got a smudge."

Casey started, then followed his gaze to her sleeve.

Swiftly she brushed the splotch away, the color merging with the black fibers of her sleeve.

She looked at her brother again, grinning.

He was still frowning, however. "I thought you were careful, Casey."

"I am!" she insisted. "I'm just feeling lightheaded today, that's all."

Sighing, she touched her forehead lightly with one hand. It was warmer than usual.

"Why are you doing this for them?" Dusty went on softly. "They're just using you, Casey. Using *us*. They don't even care if you're well enough or not—"

"Dusty, *them* is *us*," Casey interrupted him firmly. It was obvious they'd been over this topic many times before. "Once you're here, you're here to stay."

"I know," he muttered, his eyes downcast.

He shrugged finally, and then looked up. "Did you find the papers?"

She glanced at him, startled. "Papers?"

He laughed, not having missed the brief surprise in her eyes.

"I may not be as on top of things as you are, Casey, but I'm not *stupid*," he told her earnestly. "So did you get the papers?"

Casey smiled lightly, not wanting to tell her brother that the fact he was talking about Florian Lee's papers in public was proof alone that he wasn't as discreet as he could be.

"No," she had to admit, scowling. "He must have hidden them somewhere. So long as the police don't have them, we'll be fine."

"Good," Dusty murmured, closing his eyes for a moment before he tripped on a cobblestone.

He fell for a moment, but Casey caught him easily, giggling at his confused and annoyed expression.

"Anyway, I've got to report to the Boss," she reminded him. "Haven't you got somewhere you need to be?"

Two

Trisha Lee laid her folder on her desk—and realized it was her dad's. She frowned, but didn't open it; she knew her father's business was usually top-secret. Instead, she borrowed paper from her friend to last her throughout the school day, though she did get into trouble for "forgetting" her homework. That wasn't her normal, though, so it wasn't catastrophic.

At the end of the school day however, Trisha was somewhat confused when her father never showed up.

Trisha always walked to school in the morning, but her father often drove her home, unless he had something else scheduled for the day—but he hadn't mentioned anything this time. But that happened sometimes—being a detective often resulted in conflicting schedules.

Shrugging, Trisha started home alone.

When she got there, she put her hand on the doorknob, turned it a centimeter or two—and stopped. There was a tingling feeling down her spine.

Something was wrong. If Florian wasn't home, he would've locked the door—but it wasn't locked. And if he *was* home, the curtains would be drawn back to let in the afternoon sunlight.

Trisha frowned.

A sudden thought struck her, and she threw the door open, running into the dark hallway and slamming the door behind her.

She tripped on something—something—*someone*—

Horrified, Trisha picked herself up and reached for the light switch. She stared at the limp form on the floor, at the blood on the carpet—and screamed.

"Dad!"

She was on the floor, still screaming. She shut her eyes.

No. She had to know.

She opened them again. Nausea gripped her.

Her father was dead. Why? Who had done it?

Through the myriad of confused and angry thoughts, Trisha realized dimly that she should probably call the police. But right now it seemed too much.

Finally she managed to look away again, covering her face in her hands, crying her eyes red. Her whole body shook as she sobbed.

Memories of her father swarmed her mind, and they simply wouldn't stop. Trisha screamed again, remembering.

Though Trisha never known her mother, she knew Florian had meant as much to her as both parents, and possibly more. But now he was gone, and she was alone.

Alone.

Why would anyone have killed Florian? He was always so good—but his job often meant he dealt with criminals and such—

Trisha sat bolt upright. That had to be it.

She bit her lip, tears still streaming down her face. Her father must have been on a trail. And the target had…silenced him. Effectively.

Or *had* they?

Trisha's thoughts flew to the folder in her backpack—her father's—and almost without realizing, she pulled it out with trembling hands and opened it slowly.

Oh, she *was* on the right track. This was a complete report, formatted for the police.

On the first page in the folder was the name *Nelson Coligny*, and then the words, smaller but in bold: *Mafia Leader in Manhattan.*

So it was the local Mafia who'd done this.

Trisha stared at the report long and hard, then stood up, shutting the folder with a snap.

Not even noticing the obvious chaos that spoke of a search, Trisha stepped gingerly around the form in the hallway, making her way to the kitchen, to the phone.

Two thoughts were in her mind—no, three. The police had to know about this. She had to give them the folder.

And she was going to find out who'd done this.

* * *

"Daddy, there's someone to see you," came a young boy's voice as he popped his curly black-haired head in the door of his father's bedroom. He was five, maybe six. "Big girl—calls herself Cassn'da Sicko—"

The man stood up immediately from where he was pushing something under his bed, and he walked hurriedly over to the door, rumpling his son's hair fondly as he passed him.

"Thanks, Antonio. Stay inside, will you?"

"Okay," the boy returned, his buoyant expression deflating somewhat.

But then he ran off down the hallway. "Magdalena! There's a—"

The sound ended abruptly, at least to his father's ears, when the adult stepped out the front door into the crisp summer afternoon and shut the door behind him.

He glanced around briefly, then nodded to the young woman standing on the bottom step of the house.

She shook her head. "The papers were nowhere, Mr. Coligny, but Lee is taken care of. He won't be bothering us again."

"Good, and bad." The Mafia leader smiled grimly. "We need those papers."

Casey shrugged. "Sorry, but that's not my department, Mr. Coligny. You know very well that I do the job and others follow up."

He nodded a couple of times, smiling pleasantly this time. "Yes, that's right. Well, so long as the police haven't got the papers—which they haven't, seeing as they haven't shown up here yet."

Nelson Coligny laughed lightly, but then looked at Casey again, his face suddenly serious. "How are you and Dusty holding out?"

Casey smiled back. "We're good," she assured him. "How about you and yours?"

Nelson nodded again, but then he confided that he'd have to hurry back in or his two children would probably be getting into trouble.

Commending Casey for a job well done, he disappeared inside, leaving Casey to make her way to the apartment she and her younger brother shared.

Three

Casey was walking down the street a few weeks later when she was bumped into by another darkly dressed person. The man winked at her, muttered a muffled "Sorry" in Italian, then dropped a small piece of paper and dashed off, not meeting her gaze again.

Casey tensed, her eyes flashing fire as she fought the urge to go deal with the person, but then her dark eyes lit on a couple of policemen standing by the street intersection ahead.

Biting her lip, she dismissed the thought, though perhaps with a mental reminder to have words with the person next time she met him.

Bending down casually after another discreet glance around, Casey scooped up the snip of paper, dropping it into her pocket and walking off as if nothing had happened.

A few streets away, however, where there were no policemen in sight, Casey leaned against a brick wall, ignored by all the traffic.

She retrieved the note from her pocket and scrutinized it.

1800 at the pub. Dress fancy.

That was all, but it was enough to make Casey sigh and mutter something about how she never got a long enough vacation.

Silently she tore the note to pieces, then straightened away from the wall and glanced at her watch. It was 5:24; she had half an hour to get home, dress for business, and meet whomever at the pub.

* * *

No one at "the pub" was surprised to see the young woman who now leapt lightly up the steps, wearing a tattered, dark hat pulled down low over her face and a leather jacket a couple of sizes two big for her.

As she strode into the darkly lit main room of the building, her dark eyes assessed the premises as if she owned them. Stepping purposefully over to a small table in a dim corner, she pulled out a chair and sat down.

There was someone else already at the table, a short and stocky man whose Italian blood was very apparent in his dark hair, dark eyes, and olive-toned skin.

He smiled briefly at the newcomer—then his smile dropped.

"You look like you've been in a fight."

"You said dress fancy," Casey retorted calmly. "What's the game?"

Ignoring the question for the moment, the Manhattan Mafia leader took a sip of whatever was in his mug, gesturing towards Casey once he'd swallowed.

"Want anything?" he asked her.

He didn't have his bodyguards with him, Casey noticed. Probably because she was one of them herself.

She shook her head. "I don't touch alcohol and you know it. Bad for the nerves."

Nelson grinned. "Good enough. Well, then, to business. I expect you already know what the deal is?"

"Mr. Coligny, there's only one reason you've ever asked to talk to me in the past five years, and that's when you have a job for me," Casey retorted stiffy. "'Course I know. Who's the lucky target?"

Nelson shook his head. "The *who* is not important, but the job is urgent—"

"—Which is why you sent Luca to bump into me, when he knows very well I hate being bumped into," Casey interrupted, her eyes flashing. "So—"

"Yes, well this case is *urgent* urgent," Nelson went on, glancing at his watch. "You've got…four hours."

Casey shrugged. "Knife away then."

Nelson leaned forward slightly, his drink forgotten as his voice dropped to a low, quiet whisper that only Casey could hear.

"One of us is planning to defect. They've arranged to meet the cops at ten o'clock tonight—here."

He handed her a snip of paper, and Casey glanced at it a moment. It was an street address.

"Inside or outside?" she questioned.

"Outside. You have to stop them before they spill anything," Nelson went on as Casey folded the paper slowly and stored it safely away in her pocket. "Silence them, then get out of there."

He paused, watching her. "Can you do that for me, Casey? I asked the Venucci brothers, but they said it was too dangerous, what with the cops right there and all."

He bit his lip. "Well?"

She shrugged breezily. "I can do it, sure as knife. Who's the rat?"

"I can't tell you," Nelson admitted. "If the gang finds out, there'll be trouble. That's why I need you to act fast."

Casey's eyes narrowed into slits.

"You know I keep secrets," she returned somewhat indignantly. "What's different this time?"

But Nelson merely shook his head again. "Sorry."

Casey was ready to press the point, but then she noticed a few other gang members standing up as well and approaching the table. Casey's face didn't change, but one of her hands flew to her belt.

Nelson merely looked up as the three came nearer. He glanced at one of them, and his eyes narrowed.

"Luigi, what's up?" Nelson asked, even as his hand slipped to the holster in his belt, at nearly the same moment as Casey's went to her knives.

The tallest and strongest looking gangster only smirked at the Mafia leader as he glanced from Nelson's face to Casey's and then back to Nelson's.

"My oh my, *another* murder?"

His two friends snickered.

The corners of Casey's mouth curved up into a tiny smile. "I can make that four, sure as knife. I don't care."

Luigi ignored the subtle threat. "Come on, Boss, what's going on? Do you even know how to run this gang? First the notice earlier, and then now it looks like you're changing your mind—"

He stopped short suddenly as Nelson stood up.

"You got a problem with a notice?" the gang leader demanded casually.

Casey had heard nothing about any notice, but she just watched silently as Luigi sneered at Nelson.

"You don't need to play games, Nel. We all know that the only reason you're still Boss is because of your pet assassin."

Nelson had to smile. "Makes a lot of sense to me."

"Yeah, well—" Luigi cut short suddenly as Casey turned to glance at him, still smiling lightly.

"Is that supposed to be some sort of challenge?"

Luigi glanced at his two confederates, who nodded. He nodded then, as well.

"Yeah, it is."

Casey shrugged. "Good, because a challenge is something I can ignore. See you, guys. I'll take that job, Boss," she added, glancing at Nelson, who smiled and nodded.

One of the gangsters stepped into her path as she started walking toward the pub door. His hand shot out, holding a knife, but Casey flicked it aside easily.

The blade clattered to the floor just as the gangster did the same thing, launched five feet by a powerful kick from the assassin.

He knocked a table over as he hit the ground, but Casey ignored him, stepping delicately over the knife and marching out of the building, a casual smile flitting across her face.

* * *

"Where are we going, Daddy?" Nelson's son Antonio asked him curiously as the man rushed his two children, five-year-old Antonio and fourteen-year-old Magdalena, into the car about an hour later, their belongings packed.

Magdalena was curious as well, but she knew somewhat more about her father's unusual job than Antonio did, and so she was quiet—for now, anyway.

"We're going on vacation for a little while," Nelson replied, smiling as he buckled the child into a car seat. "Not far. We're just going camping."

"Camping?" the boy echoed excitedly. "Where?"

"You'll see," Nelson returned smoothly, glancing towards where Magdalena had already buckled herself in.

She was a quiet and pensive girl, with dark hair and eyes like her father and brother, though her skin was slightly lighter. She returned her father's gaze, but didn't smile.

"Anything wrong?" he asked her quietly.

She shook her head. "No. How long will we be gone?"

Nelson shrugged. "I don't know. A few days, probably. Hey, I need you two to promise something," he added quickly. "Magdalena, Antonio—this is important."

Magdalena's eyes met his, and after a moment of silence, she nodded. "Okay."

"There may be some people after us," Nelson went on seriously. "I don't want you kids getting hurt, so I'm going to leave you guys somewhere for a few days. Maybe a week. I want you to change your names for a bit—it'll be a fun game—and we'll pretend we've lived there for a very long time. Magdalena's in charge until I get back."

He grinned. "What do you think?"

"Sounds fun!" Antonio exclaimed, his face all alight.

Magdalena smiled slightly. "Okay."

"Good, then." Nelson went around the car to the driver's seat, and sat down, starting the engine. "Let's go!"

* * *

Casey was on her way back to her and Dusty's apartment when she heard a commotion break out nearby her in the street, and turned to see a small crowd of roughly dressed men talking angrily among each other across the street.

She stopped a few seconds to watch, while keeping an eye out for the cops. Her eyes narrowed as she recognized a couple of the hoodlums.

When would they learn that open brawling never got anyone anywhere?

She sighed as a fight began to break out—then tensed as the crowd fell back slightly and she could see the person in the middle of the ring, stumbling back from a hard hit.

Short, blond-haired, dark-eyed—the young man was her brother, Dustyn.

Casey was among them in an instant, scattering them as quickly as a hurricane if not as devastatingly.

A couple of seconds later the crowd had cleared away from the two siblings. Panting, Dusty grinned up at his sister, his eyes shining in a wordless thanks.

She growled. "What were they bothering you about now?"

He shrugged. "I dunno really."

"Well, come on, let's go home. I have to be somewhere in a couple of hours," Casey explained as she rushed him along after brushing off his clothes meticulously.

"Yeah, so do I," Dusty admitted. "Two messages and—"

"Then let's hurry!" Casey urged.

She didn't miss the half-wary, half-desperate glance he cast at her, and stared back openly. "What's wrong?"

"Nothing," he muttered, but then he formed one of his hands into a fist and smashed it into his other, open palm, and Casey knew it was not nothing.

"I'll tell you later," he decided finally, biting his lip and refusing to meet her gaze.

She gave him a friendly little push that nearly knocked him over.

"You silly, you can keep your secrets to yourself if they make you so gloomy," she told him wryly.

He managed a grin. "Okay, then."

"But you still have to cheer," Casey added.

Despite her saying that, a thoughtful look came over Dusty's face.

"Casey, when are we gonna get our own little place out in the mountains? You know, like we decided we'd do when we were little?"

She shrugged. "I dunno if that'll ever happen, Dusty. We're here for good."

"No, don't say that," he pleaded, looking at her imploringly.

Casey frowned, and sighed. "You know it's true—but hey, Dusty, we'll be fine, so long as we have each other. We always have, sure as knife. You know that."

"Yeah." He nodded, swallowing tightly. "So long as we have each other."

Four

Two hours later, around nine o'clock, a back alleyway in downtown Manhattan was relatively deserted, except for the random tramp and possibly a raccoon or so, searching the trash bins in hopes of finding a tasty scrap or two.

What with the ordinary noises of night—distant honking and such from other, nearby roads—the tramp didn't notice the shadowy figure that crept into the alley, but the raccoons did, and they left discreetly.

The shadow slipped through the gloom to a ladder on the side of some small, one-story shop sandwiched in between a car rental and a pet shop, and slowly and silently mounted the rungs till it decided it was high enough, and there it stopped, waiting.

Half an hour later, the police made their appearance: two of them arrived on foot, looking around themselves cautiously with their flashlights. Seeing them, the tramp hastily but unobtrusively shuffled away into the darkness.

Ignoring the tramp, the two policemen melted into the darkness around the street lamp; their flashlights were turned off, and the street seemed silent, dark, and empty once more.

It was another full thirty minutes before yet another person made his appearance: a booted, cloaked, hooded figure dressed completely in black, with a mask covering the lower half of his face.

Alone, he approached the lamp post slowly, glancing about him as if he were afraid he was being watched.

As he reached the post, one of the police officers stepped forward, and then the other. They stared at him, and he stared back.

Finally the hooded stranger's mask twitched as he opened his mouth to speak.

Then a knife materialized out of the darkness, slicing through the air and finding its way to the victim's throat as a matter of course.

The police jumped back, startled; then, as the stranger began to topple over, one of them had the presence of mind to grab hold of him and ease him to the ground gently.

While his companion radioed headquarters for an ambulance and more police, the first police officer pushed the victim's hood up and pulled his mask down, to reveal dark eyes and blond hair, light olive skin, and bloodless lips that were gasping for air.

The policeman realized with a burst of shock that the stranger had to be less than eighteen. Maybe sixteen.

He tried desperately to stop the bleeding and suffocation somehow, but it was impossible.

Twice the boy's lips moved urgently in an attempt to form words; but both attempts failed.

In seconds, his breathing went from frantic to panicked as his eyes slammed shut.

He shuddered once, and then it was over.

The policeman sighed, standing up and shining his flashlight all around, searchingly, his gun at the ready. There was no one to be seen, so he stood still, waiting for his friend to finish reporting.

Casey—for of course it was she—would normally have chosen these brief seconds to melt safely away, after notching her knife handle as a matter of course, but this time she wanted to know who the defecting traitor was.

Perhaps rashly, perhaps drawn by a sense of fate, she made her way down the ladder; the policeman's voice covered her descent completely. Softly she approached, staying out of range of the flashlight and stopping when she judged she was close enough.

The policeman was moving his flashlight around the ground near the fallen body, but finally, just as Casey was getting impatient, he turned, and the beams played over the boy's face. Casey looked—and saw—and froze.

It was Dusty.

She couldn't believe it. Casey was frozen in shock.

The look on the face was a nightmare. Twisted in pain, yet somehow peaceful and knowing. Like he knew who'd killed him and he forgave her for that.

And of course he'd known, Casey realized—he was her *brother*.

He *would* have known it was Casey, even in the exact moment he felt the knife. He would have known it couldn't be anyone else.

And he had died like that—knowing it was she, Casey—

The *boss* had known.

He'd *used* her. And for something like this—!

Why had she done it? She should've made him tell her the name. And then she wouldn't have done it. It was Nelson's fault!

But even as she tried to tell herself it wasn't her fault, she knew it was. And the knowledge was simply too much.

She had fallen to her knees now, her hands rigid at her sides, her eyes staring blankly at her brother's face even when the flashlight moved away from it.

That was how the police found her.

Casey made no resistance when they searched her and came to the conclusion that she was probably the one who'd thrown the knife, after comparing it to the others in her belt.

They confiscated it and got her into their car.

There was no reaction.

The two officers in the front of the vehicle talked quietly among themselves, only occasionally glancing back at the silent, immobile redhead who made no movement except for an occasional blinking.

Even when they got her into a prison cell—temporary, local arrangements— she would neither eat nor drink. She just sat there, sitting on the bunk, staring blankly into space, no sign of life in her eyes, sleeping occasionally, saying not a word.

Sometimes her dry, cracked lips moved. Sometimes she would shut her weary eyes, but only for a moment.

Then they would fly open with a brief, short-lived spark of life that died almost immediately.

She passed two days like that. On the third, she had visitors.

"Miss, we don't know who you are, and what your motives were. But something you've got to know—the kid is dead," one of them told her, a short, concerned-looking officer.

Nothing. No response. She didn't even look at them. The officer gave a little shrug.

His confederate took over, clearing his throat. "Also, in the last few years, there have been numerous reports of anonymous murders carried out the same way this one was. So you ought to know to expect some questioning on those as well."

Still nothing.

"Naturally, you probably didn't do this on your own," the officer admitted. "So, if you 'fess up, things ought to be easier on you."

At this point he could see he wasn't going to get any kind of answer, no matter what he did.

His shoulders slumped in defeat as he made a signal to his friend. They left the cell, being careful to lock it behind them.

"Completely useless," the first one muttered. "At this point, she's going to starve herself to death."

"Well, obviously we aren't going to let her do that," spoke the other. "But the way she acts…"

"No way her trial will do anything for her," the first officer agreed. "But according to the evidence, she's really and truly guilty. Well, she gets moved to the main city prison tomorrow for questioning. We'll see how it goes, I guess."

"So we will, hey?"

Five

T he next morning found the young, red-haired prisoner being escorted, handcuffed and under close guard, out the police station doorway and into a waiting police van.

Not a few people stood waiting, hoping to recognize her, as the police still hadn't been able to put a name on her. No one did.

Casey ignored the stares and allowed herself to be shoved into the back seat of the van, her hands limp in her lap with the handcuffs and her sharp chin tilted upwards slightly as she stared directly ahead out of dead, lifeless, dark blue eyes.

She was buckled in, the doors secured—and the van lurched into motion.

Casey swayed slightly as they went over a bump in the road; then she seemed to recollect herself a little, and dropped her gaze down to her wrists.

It stayed that way for most of the long drive. If anyone was ever uninterested in their surroundings, it was Casey. When the crash came she wasn't expecting it in the least.

Nobody was. It was too sudden, as most crashes are.

They were at an intersection when another, larger van shot into the front of the police one, sending both vehicles spinning wildly, and within seconds those drivers who hadn't slammed on their brakes immediately found themselves in the middle of a giant, destructive accident.

The two worst cars were the vans, however, and when they burst into flames only seconds after coming to a stop, the panic and confusion was so widespread that no one noticed the thin, handcuffed prisoner dragging herself out of the flaming vehicle. She got a short distance away, rolling to beat out the flames in her clothing.

Finally they were out, though her hands and face were cut and dirty from the road, and smudged and scorched from the fire.

She lay there, breathing heavily, her eyes shut, as around her people yelled and shouted and cars honked and sirens whirred.

She sighed almost unconsciously. Maybe…maybe she would die there, even as she survived.

Suddenly her eyes flashed open. A flame in them flickered for a moment as it stared at the other flames and then grew stronger.

She waited for a few moments, watching as fire trucks arrived on the scene first of all and began to tackle the flames.

Soon, the police arrived as well, though it was quite a few minutes before they began looking for Casey.

And then they found that she had disappeared.

* * *

"Really expert how y'got away, Casey. Never woulda thought. But why'd y'let 'em take ye in the first place?" the man asked frankly, filing away at the handcuff on Casey's left hand. Her right was already free.

"My business is my own," Casey retorted stiffly, holding her hand out on the table rigidly while clenching her right. "But may I ask why the Boss sent out a notice a few days ago? What was it about?"

"Oh, 'e was worried that someone was gonna rat on us and we'd have to lie low for the time bein,'" her Mafia friend told her readily. "But 'pparently it never happened."

"I see." Casey's dark blue eyes glinted hard and cold.

"And there y'go," her friend went on, holding up the second handcuff triumphantly a moment later. "Tole ye it'd be only a few minutes, didn't I, hey?"

"So you did," Casey returned distractedly, standing up.

She glanced at herself in an old, cobwebby mirror across the ramshackle room, and frowned. "Got somewhere I can clean up?"

Two minutes later Casey was back in the main room of the small, shady building, having washed her face and dampened her hair so it would stay out of her face. She twisted it into a small bun, then inspected herself again. Her deadpan expression didn't change.

"Look great," the other gangster spoke up from the corner where he was storing the handcuffs away somewhere.

He'd stopped to glance at her inquisitively. "Good as new, Casey. Want lunch?"

"Not now, but soon," Casey replied absentmindedly, suddenly turning away from the glass and looking around the room.

"Hey, Marc, didn't I leave a bundle with you last time I was here?"

"So y'did," Marco acquiesced immediately, pointing to a set of drawers across the room. "Bottom right."

"Thanks," Casey murmured, walking over to it quickly. She pulled the small drawer open, and drew out a tightly bound bundle.

The clothes she was wearing now were burnt and tattered. Casey smiled slightly as she unwrapped a new set of tights, skirt, belt, hoodie shirt, and high-collared leather jacket—and six knives.

Taking the bundle to the restroom where she'd washed up, she changed into the new clothes quickly, then bunched up her prison clothes under the sink.

The knives she slid carefully into her belt, underneath the jacket, all but one. She stared at it a moment, at her reflection in the cold, gray, dead steel.

Marco was in the tiny kitchen when she next emerged from the restroom, twirling her sixth blade expertly as well as absently in her hands.

He glanced at her momentarily, then sort of shrugged and went back to whatever he was doing.

"Lunch is tuna sandwiches and lemonade," he announced, keeping his eyes on his hands and avoiding Casey's gaze. "Ye gotta eat sometime, girl."

"I'm not hungry, right now at least, but I do need something from you,"

Casey admitted, still twirling the knife. "Have you seen the Boss lately?"

"The Boss?"

Casey's knife suddenly flicked out, catching Marco in the shoulder as he turned and pinning him against the wooden wall.

He stared at her, his mouth open in a sort of unfinished scream, and then looked down at his shoulder in shock as the blood started to trickle down his shirt.

"Yeah, the Boss. Coligny." Casey's voice was hard and cold, and her searching gaze burning and unflinching as she looked Marco directly in the eye.

"I—he—er—" Marco stuttered.

"Just tell me where he is." Casey's hand went casually to her belt, and suddenly in a swift, fluid movement she was directly in front of Marco, another knife at his throat. "Now."

Marco gulped nervously. "I don't know—"

Casey shook her head. "I said now."

"Casey, what're y'doin'—"

Marco broke off as the knife pressed harder against his throat.

"Last I heard he was at home! Y'*know* where he lives!"

"Yes, I know where he lives," Casey repeated slowly, still staring at the older gangster's terrified face. "Sure as knife."

Marco felt the knife prick his skin.

"Casey, let me go. What're you doing?" he demanded again, his heart racing. "What am I doing?"

Casey finally smiled, a smile that chilled her friend's blood.

"I'm going to get revenge for Dusty, that's what. Every one of the Mafia is going to go."

Her voice was dangerously quiet. "So, sorry, Marco. Nice knowing you."

Marco didn't reply. He didn't get a chance to.

Seconds later, Casey retrieved the knife she'd thrown, and wiped them both on the corpse's clothing, a faraway look in her dark eyes as she closed Marco's.

"There were two hundred thirty-six of us last month. Two hundred thirty-four now," she whispered to herself as she replaced the knives in her belt, notching one of them with an air of habit. "Two hundred thirty-four left, that is."

Snatching up her bundle of clothing and heading for the front door of the building, Casey glanced down at her belt. "Should be enough to do the job."

* * *

A set of six knives definitely seemed capable of doing the job, especially when wielded by Cassandra Sicario, renowned Manhattan Mafia assassin.

Her former confederates soon found that out, beginning with the discovery of Nelson Coligny's body at his flat, dead and horrendously mutilated. The remains of his bodyguards told much the same story.

That began a reign of terror in Manhattan, a singular one in that it raged against the Mafia alone and entirely, and a not-so-singular one in that the police were completely powerless over the situation.

Gangsters were found dead left and right, every one of them knifed.

The police knew the culprit was the girl who had escaped; the murderer was extremely careless about fingerprints. But they still didn't know her name—until now.

"It's Cassandra Sicario," one man told them, who'd turned himself in rather than face the certain prospect of being caught by the assassin. He had literally begged for the protection of a prison cell. "She's always been the Boss's favorite. But now she's turned on us."

"Do you know why?" the man was asked. He was so eager to spill everything he knew that the police were soon able to piece together the story for themselves—as near to Casey's point of view as they could get it.

But that didn't change the fact that she was a hunted serial killer, and neither did the incident that the self-surrendered gangster was murdered in prison a couple of days later—knifed.

The police were hunting for Casey, and soon even the FBI got called in. The girl seemed to arrive, kill, and vanish like a puff of smoke, and no one could stop her.

But then, suddenly, it stopped.

It *all* stopped.

The one hundred thirty-odd gangsters who had neither been killed nor turned themselves in, suddenly found that they could breathe again, that they were granted another day or so of life.

Sweet, wonderful life. It was a blissful feeling after having someone like Casey almost certain to kill you, one way or another.

But where *was* she?

The police didn't know, either. Search as they would, they found nothing and no one. And gradually, months later, they came to regard the case as closed. Cassandra Sicario seemed permanently gone, and for the good of Manhattan.

Slowly the city learned to relax again. Slowly, too, the Mafia regrew, keeping the police force busy as usual.

And then, weeks later, one was brought in for interrogation. A stocky, heavy-built man covered in tattoos, with dark eyes and face, who would say nothing until they asked him about Casey.

"Casey! Cassandra Sicario!" he spat, making one of the policemen step back in disgust. "I killed her! We all did! She tried to kill us but we were too many—and so we killed her instead! I did it! We're all safe now!"

He stopped for breath, ignoring the policemen's glances of doubt and incredulity.

Then his face suddenly sobered. "Actually, it wasn't me. *I* didn't kill her. It was—"

And he stopped, glancing around as if there was a ghost behind him.

It was in vain that the police pressed him for more information; he absolutely refused. But, relieved, the police figured they could assume he was right about the only thing he'd emphatically asserted: Casey was dead.

They knew nothing about a tall, dark blue-eyed, red-haired, and scarred young woman who was waking up just about then, in a tiny, poorly outfitted though neat bedroom in the extreme suburbs of Manhattan.

Six

She was staring aimlessly up at the leaky old ceiling, her half-closed dark blue eyes void of any life as she blinked slowly, perhaps wondering what she was waking up for.

Had someone called her name?

Or maybe she was awake because the bit of light that found its way around the dark hoodie shirt pinned over the window seemed more of an afternoon light than a morning one.

Whatever the reason for waking up, it obviously wasn't a good one, because she still felt more than half asleep. She blinked at the ceiling absently as the sound of gentle rainfall tapping on the roof soothed her back to sleep.

She didn't see the drop of water forming on the leaky ceiling directly above her face, or else it didn't register. At least, it didn't register until the water dripped—directly onto the apex of her sharp nose, rolling quickly down the side of her nose and then her cheek to the once-white but now patched pillow—

The girl sat up suddenly in bed, breathing hard, every muscle in her body alert and tense.

Her hand flew up to her face, brushing the tiny drop of water away. She paused with her hand still near her left cheek, and touched it again wonderingly, tracing the borders of a hard, scratchy area of skin.

A scar, reaching from the edge of her left eye to her jaw.

She winced.

A thought seemed to strike her, and she touched the top of her head with both hands, brushing the longish bangs out of her face and then feeling the curve of her hair, all the way down to her waist. It was somewhat tangled; when she held out a handful in front of her face, she could see it was a dark, auburn red color.

She traced the slope of her face down to the curved chin, and then shoved the thin, worn blanket away, glancing down at herself.

She blinked in surprise, noting that everything she wore was black. Tights, skirt, shirt. A hoodie shirt, like the one over the window. She had a belt, too, that looked like it was made to hold something, but it was empty. And boots. She was wearing boots in bed, and her eyebrows shot up at the irregularity of that.

But then they furrowed in puzzlement, a puzzlement that only grew stronger and stronger as she looked around, regarding her surroundings curiously.

The room was small, with the bed taking up most of the space. There was only the one window, the one with the aforementioned jacket in place of a curtain. The ceiling was lined with cracks, which explained how the rain had dripped through to wake her up; another drop was already forming. The walls were mostly bare, as was the floor.

If the place hadn't looked so run-down, it might have been a hospital room. And if the door hadn't opened just then without a knock, admitting a dark-haired, cheery-looking girl of about fourteen with an optimistic light in her eye and a spring in her step.

She was carrying a steaming bowl, and a cup; but as she saw the older girl sitting up, she paused and grinned embarrassedly.

"Sorry, if I'd known you were awake I would've knocked," she assured the girl in the bed quickly, leaving the cup and bowl on the chest of drawers and coming quickly over to the bed.

The older girl drew back in surprise, but didn't protest, as her youthful nurse touched her forehead tentatively.

Then the second girl winked broadly.

"Your fever's gone!" she cried jubilantly, beaming rays of sunshine down upon her still very confused-looking patient.

"I'm Emma," the fourteen-year-old went on, still grinning, "and I've been looking after you for the past two months. James and I have, I mean. James is my younger brother. He's six. Who are you?" she demanded breathlessly, and without waiting for an answer, went on: "And how'd you get hurt like that?"

The older girl shook her head slowly, looking dazed.

"I...who am I?" she asked in turn, touching her face self-consciously.

Emma laughed. "I don't know, though James has been calling you Renée, so—"

She stopped short suddenly, staring at the young woman, and her own face grew sober.

"Wait, you mean to tell me you don't know who you are?"

The red-haired stranger shook her head again. "No... But Renée works, I guess, if you don't know. Where am I?"

"Manhattan, New York," Emma told her, regaining some of her cheerful, bouncy attitude. "How'd you get here—oh, yeah. Sorry."

Renée managed a crooked grin. "Well, how'd I get here? You would know better than I would."

Emma sighed inaudibly, reaching for the bowl—its contents turned out to be soup.

"Eat," she commanded Renée, as she placed the bowl in her hands and the redhead stared at it in bewilderment. "So, what happened, is—"

"This is really good," Renée interrupted suddenly to note aloud, her spoon halfway to her mouth for a second, ravenous bite. "Did you make it?"

"I did," Emma admitted, blushing. "Glad you like it!"

"Mm," Renée nodded appreciatively, but hungrily as well as she spooned away. "Go on," she added through a mouthful, a moment later.

Emma repressed a remark about manners and went on with the story instead. "Well, James and I found you a couple of months ago. We found you...in a gutter not far from here. You know, the side-of-the-road type of thing. You were just...there. Completely knocked out, with your cheek bleeding there—" she pointed at the scar "—and a big bruise on the back of your head. I think it's gone now."

"Me, too," Renée agreed, touching the back of her head gently and feeling nothing unusual.

"Good," Emma grinned. "So, seeing as it was after dark and you looked pretty cut up, we decided to take you home—"

"All by yourselves?" Renée gaped, and Emma nodded silently.

"Yeah," she breezed over it a moment later. "Well, we've just been taking care of you since, but that's all. You've woken up a few times before, but not like this. It's good to see you awake!"

"Yeah," Renée began to say, but then the door drew open, and a little boy ran in.

He looked about six, dressed in gray rompers and a bright red shirt, barefoot, with curly, longish black hair and light blue eyes like Emma. His clothes were rather soaked, and there was an anxious expression on his face as he blurted out, "Emma! The rain's drowning the garden—"

He broke off , staring at Renée.

"You're awake!" he breathed, an expression of pure awe, wonder, and delight coming over his face as he ran over to the bed. "Renie! You're *awake!*"

"Back off," Emma warned him quickly as he showed emphatic signs of being about to jump on the bed.

"James!" she added, seeing that the six-year-old was also showing emphatic signs of not listening to her.

Scowling, the boy fell back, still staring at Renée curiously.

"That's your brother?" the redhead questioned, though it was fairly obvious.

"Yeah, I'm her brother," James replied before Emma could, nodding his head eagerly. "Who are you? I named you Renie but Emma says you probably have a real name and it's not that—"

"It's Renée, not Renie," Emma cut in shortly. "And she doesn't remember."

She fixed her brother with a very stern look. "Also, she's probably tired—"

"No, I'm not," Renée interrupted, smiling at them both. "Hey, Emma, what do I look like, by the way?"

Emma hesitated. "Well, you've got red hair and dark eyes," she said finally. "And your skin is a light olive, but it wasn't that light when we found you.

And—"

"And this?" Renée questioned, touching her left cheek.

"Yes, that's a scar." Emma shifted from one foot to the other uncomfortably. "I don't know how you got it—"

"It's fine," Renée broke in hastily. "I was just wondering what it looked like."

Emma lifted one hand, her eyes sparkling. "Hold on—I'll get you a mirror."

She disappeared out the door, and James promptly dived onto the bed, grinning mischievously at Renée. She rumpled his hair absentmindedly.

"Where'd you guys find me?" she wondered aloud, gazing straight into his frank and open blue eyes.

"By the side of the road," he answered immediately. "It was dark out but Emma and I were taking a walk. Night walks are fun, and I found you first!" His excitement seemed genuine, even if his thought process might have been a bit jumpy.

"You did?" Renée chuckled. "Was there anyone else around?"

His eyes narrowed. "Nah, it was just you. Emma wouldn't really let me see you, though, not at first. I think you were hurt bad," he confided, climbing into her lap. "But Emma fixed you up. She's a good nurse. She gave me a band-aid last week when I skinned my knee!" he grinned trustfully.

"I see," Renée smiled, though distractedly. "Where are your parents? You two have parents, right?"

That was when James's face fell, for the first time.

"No," he replied softly, shaking his small, curly-topped head mournfully. A shadow came into his eyes, and he wouldn't meet Renée's gaze. "Mom's been gone a long, long time. And Daddy—he died," he told her simply. "Three months ago, about, I think."

Renée's face contorted in real sympathy. "Oh, I'm sorry, that's awful," she murmured, wrapping her arms around the little boy as he looked like he was about to start crying. "I'm sorry I asked."

"It's okay, I guess," he mumbled gruffly, "but Emma doesn't want to talk about it, so don't ask her. How old are you, Renie? Can I call you Renie?"

"You can," Renée acquiesced, closing her eyes thoughtfully. "I don't know how old I am. How old you think I am?"

"Oh, old," he decided immediately, bouncing away from her on the bed and sizing her up. "Forty at least."

"Hmm, maybe not." Renée had to smile. "Emma said you're six?"

"Yeah, I'm six," he beamed, puffing out his chest. "I turned six last week! Emma says I'm a big boy now!"

"You certainly are," the redhead agreed emphatically, nodding.

She raised her hand quickly to cover a yawn, just as Emma came back in the room with a small, slightly tarnished hand mirror. Her eyebrows shot up as she saw that James was on the bed after all, but otherwise she made no comment as she handed the item to Renée.

Renée glanced at herself briefly, wincing as she took in the scar. It was bigger than she'd thought it was.

The rest of her face was new, too; at least, she couldn't remember it. Yes, her hair was an auburn color. Her eyes were a dark blue, she discovered; her skin, an untanned olive, as Emma had told her. Her chin was sharp, and now, as she frowned at her own reflection, she couldn't help but notice the almost haunting look in her eyes.

She wondered why it was there, and that brought back the question: *Who was she?*

She handed the mirror back to Emma, and the bowl, too, then slipped out of bed, staring down at her tight-fitting leather boots. She felt tall, probably over six feet.

Blinking twice, she glanced back at Emma and James, realizing with a start that she was much taller than Emma—and James, of course.

They, in turn, looked up at a tall, scarred young woman probably only a couple of years younger than twenty, with hauntingly void dark blue eyes that seemed to be full of meaning, just clouded over. She was slightly thin, and her face was completely expressionless as she slowly began walking towards the door.

Suddenly she stumbled; she would have fallen if she hadn't grabbed the door frame just in time. She grinned down at Emma and James, and they smiled back.

"Looks like I'll need to learn how to walk all over again!"

Seven

And learn to walk she did—quickly, too. By the time it stopped raining the next evening, Renée had recovered enough to sit on the dilapidated back porch with Emma and James, munching on dinner while pensively watching the sunset and holding conversation.

Dinner was bread, thinly spread with butter of which the color was dubious. Renée glanced hard at it before she munched away, chewing the rather stale bread with difficulty.

James pulled faces at it, but Emma seemed to be the strong silent type, and she bit away at it determinedly. Renée watched them both, hiding a smile as she finished her own slice.

"Where'd you get this, Emma?" she asked her younger, new friend curiously.

Emma shifted uncomfortably. "Um—"

"Don't answer that," Renée laughed, grinning at her. But then she grew serious. "So you take care of yourself and James, eh. Well, you do a pretty good job."

"And she takes care of you, too!" James chuckled delightedly.

Renée ignored him, smiling lightly. "Anyway, Emma, don't take offense at this, but I'm going to find a job as soon as I'm stronger, okay?"

Their eyes met, and then finally Emma smiled slowly. "Okay. What kind of job?"

"I don't know." Having finished her bread, Renée stretched luxuriously and grinned. "Does this mean I'm adopted?"

"You, adopted?" Emma actually laughed aloud. "You look like an adult to me."

"Well, adopt me anyway," Renée told her irrepressibly, reaching out and trying to brush James's hair out of his face with her hand. He needed a haircut, and the gesture on her part was futile. James smirked cheekily at her.

"Should we, James?" Emma asked her little brother dubiously.

He nodded energetically, a movement which jerked his hair out of Renée's reach, even if it wasn't entirely on purpose. "I like Renie!"

Emma's eyebrows shot up, and she muttered something under her breath. "James, for the hundredth time—"

"It's fine," Renée assured her hastily, having obviously heard this speech before. Emma scowled, and James's face took on an expression of sweet innocence.

"Does that mean I'm accepted?" the young adult wondered a minute or two later, the two children having finished their supper as well.

Emma glanced up at her, her keen eyes searching Renée's for a moment before she answered almost grudgingly. "Yes."

"You can be our aunt!" James added enthusiastically. Emma's jaw dropped open, but before she could say anything, Renée was already refuting the proposition.

"I don't know if I'm old enough to be your aunt," she admitted ruefully, pushing her hair out of her face as a breeze floated by and made her red hair swirl around her head. She touched her scar lightly. "How old did you say I was, again?"

James turned around to look directly at her, and his little forehead furrowed thoughtfully. "I said forty. But now you don't look that old," he realized as he stared openly. "You look…ten-eleven."

"Ten-eleven, eh," Renée mused thoughtfully. "I ought to be able to get a job, then."

Emma was looking at her as well. "I'd say more like eighteen," she declared softly, and Renée nodded.

"Probably. But still old enough, right?" she grinned. Emma nodded her agreement silently.

"What kind of job?" James wondered aloud.

"Oh, I don't know," Renée began, but Emma interrupted her.

"How are you supposed to get a job if you don't like going out of the house?" she asked Renée frankly, looking her directly in the face.

Renée shrugged. "I'll manage," she replied, touching her scar softly. "Maybe I'll get a night job or something. I can wear a hoodie, probably, and it doesn't matter that much anyway," she admitted. "Maybe someone can tell me who I am."

"Renée, if we found you in a ditch bleeding and unconscious, you might not want someone to tell you who you are, or even recognize you," Emma told her seriously. "I'd stick with a night job. If you have to get a job at all—"

"Are you kidding me?" Renée laughed. "Of course I'm going to get a job. You've been taking care of James on your own for—how long now? Three months? Four?"

"Three," Emma muttered, standing up and going into the house. "Whatever," Renée heard her mumble as she closed the door behind her.

Renée glanced after her momentarily, then shrugged. "Whatever?"

"She's just quiet," James told her slowly, scrambling down off the steps to catch a cricket that had caught his fancy.

"She's been like that since we heard about Daddy," he went on, snatching up the cricket and closing his chubby hands around it eagerly. "That's why I like being around you. You're nice and funny and—" He broke off suddenly as the cricket managed to escape his grip, the boy and went after it again with a howl of annoyance.

"I see," Renée mused, resting her head on her knees thoughtfully. "So she wasn't always like that?"

"Oh, no." James regained possession of the cricket and turned to face Renée, his long black bangs shadowing his face more than usual in the twilight. "She used to be a real fun sister."

"Mhmm." Renée nodded slowly. She grinned at him. "I bet she'll be like that again someday."

"Yeah," he muttered, absorbed in observing his newfound pet try to escape him. "I bet so."

"You like bugs?" Renée chuckled, watching him interestedly.

"Yes," James admitted readily, though he was somewhat distracted. Suddenly the cricket leapt away from him again, and this time succeeded in disappearing among the long, unmoved grass and weeds. James promptly dove in after it, but a call from Renée recalled him, though reluctantly.

"Don't go in there! There could be snakes!" Renée shouted to him, jumping up and hastening over.

A moment later, James emerged, looking annoyed as only a six-year-old can. "It got away," he mumbled.

"No worries, it's better that it get away than you get bitten by a snake," Renée told him seriously. Still standing, she cast her gaze around the yard.

The grass was extremely overgrown, over three feet high and definitely tall enough to lose a small child in. It came pretty close to the one-story house, making the back steps nearly the only place of shelter. It was a depressing sight, and Renée turned her gaze to the sky.

As of late it had nearly always been blue, but now it was clouded over: heavy and overcast. Renée stared wonderingly up at it for a moment before voicing her thoughts.

"Looks like it's going to snow!"

Eight

"How did you know it was going to snow?" James asked Renée the next morning as his eyes flew from the snow, to Renée, to the snow again.

Emma laughed, sounding truly cheerful for the first time in weeks. "It's winter!"

Renée watched the pure-white snow with shining dark blue eyes, as more of it sprinkled on her head, gradually powdering her recently-cut-short red hair with white specks. "It is that," she laughed. "Sure as knife."

Neither she nor James noticed the almost startled glance Emma shot at Renée, and seconds later Renée had leapt down the porch steps and was on her knees in the snow in front of the house. She scooped up a couple of handfuls of the cold white powder, and let it fall, laughing like a baby.

"It's so cold!" she breathed, brushing her hands off and standing up again, then wiping the snow off her hair. "But there isn't much of it yet."

"There'll be more," James assured her eagerly. "There always is, Renie. Have you seen snow before?"

Renée laughed, shaking her head. "Nope!"

* * *

A week or so later, there was more snow—a good deal of it. Emma and James enjoyed that immensely, though by that time Renée had gotten her night job and was ready to hit the hay as soon as she got home each morning.

The snow hadn't fallen for long before the streets filled with shouting children. Normally there wouldn't have been that many kids out in the streets in the middle of the day, but the teachers of New York had declared it a holiday, and each child was well eager to take advantage of the fact to play outside, even if their mothers watched anxiously from the windows to make sure their darlings weren't coming into close contact with any dangerous companions—in other words, street kids.

But the shouting was so loud, and the snow so inviting, that James and Emma finally ventured out. They discovered that most of the kids had gathered into an empty lot, a few houses away from where James and Emma were staying.

At first it was just younger children, but as a few high schoolers made their appearances, the game took on a semblance of order.

Pretty soon Emma and James found themselves on opposing teams, and although for a while Emma tried to win and watch her brother at the same time, eventually she ended up devoting all her energies to the good of her team. No one knew her, and she didn't know them, but here she was anyway—recklessly snowballing away, and accurately too.

But suddenly, when she began to hear James shouting her name at the top of his lungs, she froze, listening. There was a desperate necessity in his voice, and Emma immediately forgot all about the game.

A snowball hit her directly in the face then, splattering all over her mouth and eyes and nose and hair.

Emma stood there openmouthed, still listening.

"Gotcha!" one of the other team yelled, seemingly in her face as well, though they weren't right in front of her. "You're out! Ahoy! You're out!"

No one else seemed to notice James's voice, and Emma shook her head, finally brushing the snow off her face.

"I'm not playing!" she yelled back, breaking into a run in the direction from which she'd heard her brother's voice.

Booing followed her. "Bad sport!" she was called, but Emma wasn't paying attention anymore.

She found James behind another building, closer to their house. A couple of kids her age had hold of him and were enthusiastically discussing how they were going to wash his face. Street kids always needed a washing, right?

About six older kids looked on unconcernedly. Looking up and seeing Emma running towards them, one of the not-so-nice-looking young ladies, probably seventeen, shouted for the others to just get on with it.

"Let go of my brother!" Emma shouted, charging down the snowy lawn.

The girl kept watching her relaxedly. "Sure, why don't you let go of him yourself? We're only havin' fun—" and then she suddenly shot out her hands and grabbed Emma, just as the younger girl was seconds away from her target.

Emma fought like a wildcat, but when a couple more older kids added their strength to the girl's, she found it a hopeless struggle.

Finally she stopped, panting for breath, her hair a mess and her cheek bleeding.

"Let him go," Emma gasped out. The two kids who had James had stopped when she arrived, but now they were looking at Emma's captors nervously.

The girl laughed. She was panting herself and had a cut lip. But worse than that was the angry glint in her eyes. Emma thought the girl wanted to splatter her on the pavement or something equally drastic.

But Emma couldn't afford to be afraid. Not when James was in danger.

"Come on," the older girl urged the other kids. "Let's give him a facewashin' and then we can do her—"

"HELP!" Emma screamed suddenly, having recovered enough breath. "SOMEBODY HELP! SOMEBODY—"

She was cut off as her olive-skinned, black-haired, and older captor shoved her down in the snow suddenly and held her there.

Emma kicked back desperately. Then she realized she couldn't breathe, and kicked even harder.

The older girl held her there relentlessly. Even as Emma felt she was suffocating, she heard the girl's voice, taunting and hateful.

"I know who you are. You don't need to hide from me—"

Suddenly it stopped, and Emma found she wasn't being held down anymore.

The fourteen-year-old scrambled to her knees, coughing and spitting out snow as she gasped in giant gulps of air. Sweet, precious air.

Dimly she heard Renée's voice as the scarred redhead swirled in like a tornado, throwing Emma's and James's attackers left and right.

"Leave 'em alone!"

Emma stopped coughing and stared in shock as Renée's hidden agility and fighting talent came into view.

The scarred redhead hurled one of her assailants into the snow at her left with a sweeping, almost absentminded shove; another, the one who'd held Emma's face down in the snow, was cleared an instant later as Renée jerked her away by the back of her collar and literally threw her out of her way.

Glancing at Emma momentarily, Renée nodded to her and then went on to rescue James—an unnecessary job, since his attackers had already dispersed at the sight of the furious red-haired athlete.

Renée bent down, grabbed the little boy's hand, and helped him up, smiling encouragingly at him.

"Renie," he breathed, grinning hugely. Giggling, Renée brushed the snow off his hair and the front of his clothes.

Emma came up behind her slowly, breathing hard as she brushed herself off. "That was just in time."

"Better late than never," Renée reminded her, not losing one degree of her confident smile.

"How'd you do that?" Emma demanded, frowning.

And then Renée realized what she'd done, and she caught her breath, looking puzzled. "I—I don't know. I heard you and James yelling, and I just…"

"Well, no one's hurt," James pointed out, grabbing Renée's skirt as if the contact reassured him. "Right?"

"Sure as knife," Renée agreed, not noticing as something strange came into Emma's eyes and the younger girl caught her breath.

The young adult glanced up at the sky. Big, gray clouds were forming quickly, threatening rain—or snow.

"Let's go inside," Renée suggested, reaching down and scooping the black-haired six-year-old into her arms easily. He laughed, wriggling; but she held him anyway.

"Okay," Emma nodded, and Renée led the way back to the house the three shared.

None of them noticed that the black-haired, olive-skinned seventeen-year-old that'd shoved Emma in the snow was still there where Renée had thrown her, watching them out of hateful black eyes.

She stared at Renée, recognition dawning in her eyes. The teenager's mouth curled up in a spiteful smirk.

"*You*, too!"

Nine

That evening, as Renée prepared to leave for her night job, Emma was putting James to bed. But Renée waited for her anyway.

Finally Emma showed up, but only to glance at Renée and raise her eyebrows.

"You're going to be late," she remarked, then turned to head back towards the room she now shared with Renée.

Renée's voice stopped her in her tracks. "Emma, did you know those kids?"

Emma froze momentarily, but then seemed to recover herself. "No. At least, not personally. They seemed like the normal type to me," she added under her breath.

"Okay," Renée murmured. "Just wondering."

She stepped towards the front door, but it was Emma's turn to stop her. "What, did *you* know them?"

"No," Renée returned, slightly surprised.

Emma breathed out slowly. "I didn't think so."

"You okay?" Renée asked her, somewhat concernedly. "That girl seemed pretty violent."

"I'm fine," Emma assured her, still without turning around. "Good luck at work."

Renée yawned self-consciously. "Yes. Goodnight!"

* * *

Renée finished work at 6 AM, but she took the long way home like she usually did. Part of the reason for that was because she liked to stop along the way to carry out various, self-imposed errands. One of them—today's reason, actually—was to take a walk to steady her nerves.

Even if she didn't completely comprehend it, she knew *something* was wrong.

She didn't know what it was, this tendency to look at people—just normal, ordinary people who ignored her as they went about their business—as if she were an agent on unknown territory and might have to fend off any one of them as an enemy at any time.

She'd barely noticed the strangely defensive preparedness before, but now that she'd discovered her apparent fighting ability, it was increasingly clear. Not only was she wary of strangers, but potentially and capably hostile to them as well.

It was a new feeling, and Renée wasn't sure if she liked it.

She ended up increasing her speed, so as to be home sooner than usual and escape the early morning crowds.

Renée didn't care to be seen in public. Someone had beaten her up and left her in a gutter, after all; and Renée was willing to bet they might not be exactly friendly, if she were to run into them again.

Though she felt confident she could defend herself in such circumstances, there was one drawback: She had no idea who the enemy even was.

Eventually reaching the small house, she let herself in at the back door, replacing the key under the back step before stepping in quietly and locking the door again behind her.

She looked down the darkened hallway—they didn't have electric lights— and wondered, not for the first time, how Emma and James had gotten a place like this one. True, it was rundown and in an unsavory part of the city, but still it was much better than any other orphans had on their own.

Dismissing the perplexing question—since she'd never gotten a straight answer from Emma—Renée tiptoed down the hallway, trying not to wake anyone up.

She seemed endowed with a natural stealthiness, but in spite of that, as she stepped into the kitchen, she discovered Emma was already awake. The fourteen-year-old didn't notice Renée at all, until Renée sadly relinquished the maybe not-so-charitable idea of sneaking up on her and walked around the counter with a loud sigh.

Emma glanced up at the clock from where she was stirring a pot of oatmeal, looking almost annoyed for a moment.

"Six-thirty. Want some breakfast—I mean, dinner? It's almost ready," she assured the older girl eagerly.

Renée slowly entangled herself from her hoodie jacket, hanging it up carefully on a hook by the front door out of the kitchen. Emma was a very strict housekeeper, and Renée preferred not to antagonize her, seeing as she was now "adopted."

"Oh, sure," she grinned. "Thanks. Want help?"

"Yeah, sure, why not?" Emma finally allowed herself to smile, and she stepped away from the stove, going to wash her hands that were warm from the steam. "I'll get some strawberry jam."

"You have strawberry jam?" Renée asked, startled. She began stirring the oatmeal quickly, albeit thoroughly.

"Mhmm," Emma nodded.

"What's the special occasion?" the older redhead wondered.

Emma shrugged. "I dunno. But it'll be Christmas in a week."

Renée felt like suggesting they save the jam for Christmas, but then she got a new and better idea. She smiled to herself as Emma set the jar on the table and took three worn and chipped bowls from the cupboard, then three spoons.

"That reminds me," Renée spoke up suddenly. "I don't have to work again till three days after Christmas."

"Really?" Emma grinned. "Well, after I go to work today, I won't have to work until a week after Christmas." She smirked.

"What'll we do during our lovely, long vacation?" Renée wondered aloud.

Emma shrugged distractedly, struggling with the jar of jam. She grunted a few times in a vain effort to open it, then gave up and carried it over to the stove where Renée was. "Can you open this?" she asked simply.

Renée nodded, carefully positioning the wooden spoon atop the bubbling, steaming pot before wiping her hands on her skirt and then taking the jar from Emma. Setting it on the counter, she wrapped one hand firmly around the lid and the other around the jar, then gave it a sudden, intense twist.

The lid popped and came loose. Renée grinned, handing the jar back to Emma.

"Thanks," Emma returned, taking the jar back to the counter. Then she came back to the stove. "Is that ready yet?"

* * *

"I know what to do for vacation," James declared enthusiastically some minutes later, over a bowl of oatmeal topped with strawberry jam. He'd just woken up, and Emma ran her hands through his hair a couple of times in an effort to smooth it down. Then she sat down.

Renée was already eating, sitting opposite James, and he was looking at her when he made his announcement.

"Really?" she asked him interestedly. "Knife away."

"What if we went down to the river and got a boat ride?" he suggested eagerly.

"But the water will be freezing cold," Emma protested. "That's a summer thing."

"But..." James's six-year-old face fell.

Renée glanced at Emma, and suddenly Emma glanced back at her. Their eyes met, and Renée realized they were both thinking the same thing.

They didn't really have the money to spare on things like boat rides.

"You know what," Emma said slowly, "I heard about a free-for-all Christmas festival, the day after Christmas, downtown. I wasn't going to mention it, because it'll be after James's bedtime, but..." She hesitated.

Renée snatched at the chance immediately. "Yes, that sounds perfect!"

James could only stare at his sister and their friend, his eyes big with excitement. A Christmas festival!

Ten

That Christmas, the three assisted at Midnight Mass in the Cathedral of the Immaculate Conception, New York.

It was about 1:30 AM when they got home, and all of them straightaway tumbled into bed, but Renée lay awake for a while, thinking. She hadn't tried to go to Communion. Neither had Emma, for reasons Renée didn't know. Renée didn't know if she'd belonged to any religion before.

But she did know she wanted to become a Catholic.

Who could she be? she wondered, and why would she be so good at martial arts? And who were Emma and James? She still didn't know their surname—Emma hadn't wanted to tell her. But why had they taken Renée in, just like that?

If the two were normal "street kids," Renée was sure they were probably used to seeing homeless people, and injured ones, too. So why had they chosen Renée to adopt and nurse back to health?

She sighed. There were too many questions, and she didn't have any of the answers. Sometime, when the time was right, she'd have to confront the secretive Emma—but for now, it was probably better to leave things as they were.

Though her scar reminded her every day that she knew nothing of her past, she was grateful to be with these two children.

They were so happy—and so simple. At least James was. So sweet and gentle. And Emma was practical and ordinary. It was her very ordinary-ness that Renée liked best of all.

Renée smiled, thinking about him. Maybe in her past life there had been someone like the little boy. Or like Emma.

She wondered if she'd ever know.

Falling asleep eventually, looking out the window at the stars, Renée had no way to guess that this was going to be the last peacefully, blissfully oblivious night of her life.

* * *

"It's huge!" was James's first reaction to the giant tree set up in a square in Manhattan, decked all over with lights and tinsel. It was the evening after Christmas, and he, Emma, and Renée were at the Christmas festival downtown.

Emma stared up at it silently—Renée suddenly realized she wasn't looking at the tree, but at where it disappeared into the black sky, with a brilliant, six-pointed star to mark the tip of the tree.

James was tugging Renée's hand; he wanted to go hunt for hot chocolate, it seemed. Renée nodded to him, then glanced at Emma, sighing. She'd love to let the fourteen-year-old walk around on her own, but cities were dangerous.

"Emma," she whispered, tapping the girl's shoulder, who started and wheeled around. "We'd better stick together. James wants to get hot chocolate?"

Emma nodded briefly. "Oh, sure. I've got money for that," she winked.

"So have I," Renée grinned back.

Emma laughed, then shrugged. "We can get some more later, I guess, before we head home."

"Sure as knife!"

* * *

About an hour later, Renée couldn't help but notice that James was definitely getting cold and tired. Emma kept up a brave show of being interested in things, but it was obvious that she was tired as well. Renée gently led returning home into the conversation.

"I'm cold," she announced, rubbing her hands together. "Who wants to get more hot chocolate and then go home?"

James's face lit up in an excited six-year-old grin. "Me!"

Emma laughed silently at Renée, recognizing the older girl's tactic. "Me, too," she acquiesced. "It's getting late."

"Alrighty, then, let's head back," Renée decided, suddenly bending down and picking up James around his waist. He squealed in half-protest, half-enjoyment, as she swung him up to her shoulders and sat him there.

"Keep your hands out of my eyes and off my neck and you can stay there," she told him. "And don't pull my hair."

But it was futile, and no later than five minutes later James had—whether accidentally, or on purpose, Renée couldn't tell—sufficiently antagonized Renée to the point that she lowered him back to the ground.

"Fine," she muttered, putting her somewhat aching arms on her hips before taking James's hand with one of them, "you can walk the rest of the way. I'm not carrying a squirmy frog!"

"I'm not a squirmy frog!" he returned, aghast. But protest as he might, Renée remained adamant.

Meanwhile, Emma found the hot chocolate stand—about twenty feet away from where they were now—and began to negotiate the purchase of three foam cups of hot chocolate, most definitely with marshmallows and very warm, please—it was still snowing, harder now.

While holding tightly to James's hand so that he couldn't disappear, Renée kept an eye on Emma so that she wouldn't disappear either.

A few minutes later, the girl rejoined them, passing out cups of hot chocolate to her younger brother and her older friend.

Renée sipped hers slowly, as did the other two—it was piping hot.

They began heading in the general direction of home, and as they went, Renée fell into a sort of half-pensive, half-sleepy reverie. The voices around her—people were always talking at gatherings like this, even at eleven at night—seemed to become dull background noise, and the lights a blurry element of her surroundings.

Suddenly all that changed. Someone screamed.

Behind her.

She wheeled around instinctively, just in time to knock the knife away from the masked, darkly dressed man who had been leaping at her.

At the same moment her hand shot out—dumping the overly warm hot chocolate all over him while also knocking the knife away—her foot did too, and she kicked the man away expertly, sending him flying to the pavement some feet away.

The crowd around them cleared, watching, as the man tried to get up but fell back down after trying to stand on one of his feet. His mask had come off, and he rocked back and forth, holding his foot. Clearly it was broken.

After the initial shock of the attack and her own defense, Renée bent down to pick up the knife—and then her fingers closed around the hilt.

She stared at her hand in surprise. It fit so naturally around the blade's handle that it was almost frightening.

Then she glanced up—straight into her attacker's face.

Their eyes met, and Renée stopped breathing.

He was dark-haired, with olive skin, dressed like any typical gangster, though with hot chocolate spilled all over his front.

But his *face*. Renée knew his face, she realized.

Her eyes dilated and her pulse raced as all the memories flooded back at once.

At the same time, the would-be murderer was still sitting on the pavement, looking at the girl he'd just tried—and failed so miserably—to kill.

He saw a tall, olive-skinned, freckleless young woman of about eighteen, with waist-length, dark red hair. Her hood had fallen back, and the scar on the left side of her face was plain for all to see. As well as the completely shocked, stricken look in her eyes.

She stared back, her jaw hanging open.

The crowd stared as well, watching them. It was obvious that the girl knew her attacker, especially when she started walking towards him, still holding the knife.

Someone yelled for the police; but then she stopped, directly in front of the man, with the knife in her hand.

Suddenly he began blubbering that he hadn't meant any harm, he had a family, he wasn't trying to kill her, and so forth; but the redhead just stared, some obvious struggle going on in her mind. Her face twitched a couple of times.

And then suddenly she dropped the knife. It landed, its tip sticking in the pavement between the criminal's right index and middle fingers.

He stared at his hand for a moment; then he looked back at Renée.

"Casey," he whispered, but she had already turned around and was walking away.

Cassandra Sicario, lately known as Renée, walked away, down the street, oblivious of the few people who tried talking to her.

Emma and James followed quietly, Emma quiet and almost frightened, James wide-eyed and definitely terrified. Who would try to knife his friend Renie?

Casey was oblivious of it all until a stranger tapped her shoulder. She was a friendly-looking young adult, just over twenty, who seemed concerned.

"Are you o—" she began, breaking off suddenly as the shorter, scarred, red-haired girl wheeled around to face her, her hands coming up automatically.

Casey blinked and took in her surroundings, only to find she had just twisted some random, confused stranger's hands away from her in a defensive position.

She blinked again and dropped the girl's hands, looking as embarrassed as she could when she felt as if a bomb had just exploded over her head.

"I—I'm sorry," she whispered. "I'm sorry."

"It's fine," the girl murmured, though she didn't look convinced. "Are you okay? You should probably wait around for the police—"

"The police?" Casey interrupted, glancing around in dizzy alarm. She saw James and Emma behind her and grabbed their hands tightly as a matter of course.

"Yeah—" The girl broke off again, this time as sirens rent the air.

Casey shrugged distractedly, then her eyes filled with something very near to panic as they reflected the blue and red lights of the incoming police cars. She glanced at Emma and James. "We're gonna run. Ready?"

Eleven

❧

"Renie, what's going on?" James asked Casey for the tenth time as she led the way up the steps to the house. It was past ten-thirty now, and he was exhausted—but still curious.

Casey ignored his question as she ushered them in the front door, closing it behind them.

She stood against it, breathing lightly. "James, it's past your bedtime."

"But—" he began, even as he rubbed his eyes sleepily.

"Go to bed," Emma broke in sharply, speaking up for the first time since the incident with Renée and the anonymous knifer.

James looked like he was about to protest further, but the look Emma gave him then dashed that prospect to pieces.

Murmuring a brief, sulky "Goodnight," he glared at Emma and Casey before relenting and hugging them both, and then slipping down the hall towards his room.

The girls waited until his door shut with a click. Another sound followed as Casey turned and locked the front door.

She stood there for a moment without turning around, her hand still on the handle. A sixth sense told her when Emma moved slightly closer.

"Renée, who was that?" the younger girl whispered finally.

Casey didn't turn around, just brought her hand up slowly to touch her scar.

53

There was something in the movement that made chills run up and down Emma's spine, even though she was used to this kind of behavior.

"Renée?" she asked again, even quieter this time.

"Emma—Emma," Casey began finally, then stopped.

She turned around finally, looking hard at the younger girl. There was something new in her eyes, something Emma hadn't seen before.

"Your name is Emma?"

Emma drew breath in sharply, and then turned around without a word, walking down the hallway towards her own room.

But it was too late. Casey had seen her face, and she knew why Emma hadn't answered.

Because her name wasn't Emma. It was Magdalena.

Magdalena Coligny.

* * *

Casey sat on the edge of her bed some few minutes later, her face in her hands, her long red hair loose down her back, her day clothes still on. Changing clothes had never been farther from her mind.

The gangster… That petrified look on his face…

Everything. She remembered it all, now.

Her childhood in the Manhattan Mafia, with her younger brother Dusty. Her assassin training—taught by Nelson Coligny's older sister, a professional who was long gone now. The gang's relationship to them. Her years of working for Nelson.

Her evenings of dreamily planning ahead with Dusty for the time when they'd both be free to do as they wished. Her position as the most-feared member of their respective Mafia.

And then—that fateful day, when the world had crashed down about her shoulders. The day she'd murdered Dusty, her own brother.

A tear ran down her cheeks, and then another. Within seconds, her shoulders were shaking as she sobbed, covering her face in an attempt to keep it quiet.

She hadn't cried for Dusty before, but she did now. And not just for Dusty. For all those she'd killed as Mafia assassin and anti-Mafia assassin.

She felt crushed. She hadn't thought her past might be anything like this.

But here it was—and she didn't know how she was still alive. The police were after her, and so was the gang, in all likelihood.

How was she still alive? *Why* was she still alive, that was the question.

Suddenly she stopped crying and looked up and out the single window. It had stopped snowing, and the moon and stars were plainly visible.

Even as she stared at them, a dim light of hope began to creep into Casey's eyes.

She had been saved for a reason, she realized that now. It was no coincidence that she had been to Mass less than twenty hours ago. She was different from how she'd been before she lost her memory, she knew. Or she would have killed that gangster, right then and there.

She closed her eyes, touching her scar yet again.

She could bet Luigi da Milano was in charge now.

Emma and James were Magdalena and Antonio Coligny, the Boss's two children? Casey could hardly believe it, but…it was true.

So that was why Emma had always been so aloof. Casey could assume they didn't know who she was, that she'd been the one to kill their father.

She bit her lip at the thought of telling them. No, she couldn't.

But if the gang were after her, she couldn't stay, either, she realized. They *had* to be after her, or Cosmio Puccini wouldn't have been trying to kill her.

But how did they know she was still alive? As Renée, Casey had been taking precautions to be as little noticed as possible.

Suddenly she sat up straighter as the teenage girl who'd been holding Emma down in the snow came to mind. Casey had somehow sensed that she was no ordinary bully kid, and now she knew exactly who the girl had been.

Alessandra da Milano.

She would have told her father about seeing Casey, and he would've acted accordingly. That was probably where Cosmio Puccini came in.

And now that Cosmio had failed, others would be coming for her. If they found out where she was living.

Casey clenched her fists. If they found out...what would happen to Magdalena and Antonio?

Casey might have hated and killed their father, but she know that now, more than ever, she would have to protect his children. It was her duty.

Casey thought of going to the police, but then she frowned. What if Magdalena and Antonio were discovered before the police could take action?

No, it was just too risky. She was going to have to lead the gang away before she tried to make contact with the authorities.

The redhead winced at the thought. This wasn't going to end well for her. But she knew she had to make reparation, somehow—and keep Emma and James safe.

The red-haired, former assassin suddenly slipped to her knees, her hands folding in an instinctive gesture.

Hanging her head a moment, she took a deep breath, and then flung her gaze skyward, through the frosty window to the now-cloudy heavens beyond. Her cheeks were moist with tears, her eyes deeply sad and imploring.

"Oh God, help me," she prayed, for the first time in her life. Her vision blurred, and her voice choked. "Help me know what to do. Help me make amends. What do I do?"

There was no answer—at least, not that anyone else could've heard. But Casey heard something—or seemed to—just when the clouds were suddenly pierced to allow for a single, unusually brilliant shaft of moonlight.

It shot through the sky like an arrow, illuminating the girl's wet, scarred face. But she didn't see it. Her eyes were closed, her lips moving in silent prayer.

Everything was suddenly so clear. She knew what she had to do, and she was going to do it. She couldn't do it on her own, she knew; but she was going to have help.

"Thank you," she whispered, her voice still shaky but more calm this time. She opened her eyes, glancing up at the light. "Thank you."

Twelve

I t had been a late night for him, and so it was perhaps natural that six-year-old Antonio Coligny—previously known simply as "James"—didn't wake up as early as he usually did.

But when the morning sunlight finally pierced through the dark, misty clouds of slumber, and he opened his eyes, blinking, then hopped up to say his prayers and get dressed, he was somewhat startled to discover that only Emma—Magdalena—was in the kitchen.

She was sitting on the counter, her legs dangling as she inspected a recipe card.

As Antonio entered, she looked up and smiled distractedly at him.

"Good morning. That's for you," she added, jerking her head towards the bowl of porridge on the table.

Grinning, Antonio walked eagerly over to the table; but then, before he sat down to eat, he glanced back at Magdalena. "Where's Renie?"

She didn't look up. "She's gone."

"Gone?" Immediately the smile disappeared from the little boy's face. "Renie's gone? Where? Why?"

It was obvious from Magdalena's face that she knew more, but she wasn't going to tell him. "Just gone. She won't be back."

Antonio wouldn't have been able to read the note Casey had left behind, but it wouldn't have helped his case anyway, Magdalena thought ruefully. Antonio didn't need to know that Casey had been the one to kill their father—and that she now intended to turn herself in.

"Gone?" he said again. "Emma, we have to find her!"

Magdalena shook her head, but then, before she could say anything else, Antonio slipped down from his seat, leaving his breakfast behind as he ran impetuously towards the front door.

His hand fumbled for an instant with the lock, and then he flung the door open, disappearing outside.

"James!" Magdalena shouted after him in alarm.

His curly black-haired head flashed in the doorway for a moment. "Come on, Emma! Let's go find her!"

* * *

In an old, long-deserted apartment building near the edge of Manhattan, in the highest story, there was a small unit of rooms, which had obviously been uninhabited for at least four months, probably more.

But today, there was a human in the building, and the mice and cockroaches scuttled away out of sight as her footsteps resounded on the worn wooden floors.

She mounted the final flight of steps quietly and carefully, not bothering to use the railing.

She wore tall, black boots, as well as black tights, skirt, and hoodie jacket. The hood was pulled low over her face, though her red hair and the knife scar on the left side of her face was still visible, as well as the hard, sad look in her dark blue eyes.

She moved silently, almost like a cat. When one of the planks creaked unexpectedly under her weight, she tensed instinctively. Finally, however, she reached her destination: a blank door on the top floor.

She stood in front of it a moment, then put her hand on the knob, her face clearly doubtful. Then she tested the knob, frowning. It was locked.

Casey looked around in desperation; then her eyes lit up, and she felt around in her pockets for a moment, discovering a bobby pin. Seconds later, the lock clicked as her deft fingers worked their magic, and Casey had gained admittance to the apartment.

She looked around it for a few minutes, noting the shredded furniture and the faded, peeling wallpaper. There was nothing of interest there, and she went down the short hallway, pushing one door open to reveal what had been a girl's room at one point.

Her room.

Casey found her belongings just where she had left them, but nothing was much use anymore. She left her room and then went into Dusty's, tiptoeing into the room in an almost reverential manner.

Like hers, his room had been left neat and tidy—but a small envelope had been left on the dresser. Her dark eyes opening wide in surprise, Casey stepped over to the wooden piece of furniture, reaching out to pick up the envelope.

She hesitated half a moment, with her fingertips just over the paper; then she grasped it and opened it, completely ignoring the thick dust layer that then coated her fingers.

There was a single piece of paper inside, and Casey slowly pulled it out, staring at it for a moment before sitting down on the bed to read it.

Her eyes misted over as she read.

"Dear Casey," she read aloud, under her breath. "I'm writing this to say goodbye. I don't even know if you'll be reading this, but I sure hope you will. Sure as knife, as you'd say.

"Casey, I want to say thank you for everything. I've decided to go over to the police and tell them everything. I hope you can forgive me, but I can't go on like this. You know how I feel, Casey.

"I've told them that I'll tell them everything, if only they let you and me off lightly. It's what we've always wanted, Casey. You know you never really wanted to be in the Mafia, and neither did I. There's got to be another life for us somewhere, Casey, if only we start going straight.

"I know you'll understand, even if no one else will. I am so happy that I've decided to do this. But I'm also scared. I don't know what's going to happen. You know what we say… 'Once you're here, you're here to stay.' Can there be an exception to that? Or is it really set in stone?

"I'm going to find a way out, Casey, and I hope you can, too. Whatever happens tonight, whether it ends the way I'm hoping it will, or whether I die and everyone else…goes on, I hope you find a way out. I'm probably going about this the wrong way. I'm stupid, and you know that only too well.

"But this is the best I can think of. I'll try my best, Casey. Good luck.

"I love you, and God bless. This is goodbye for now. *Dusty.*"

Casey stared at the paper, at what were probably the last words her brother had ever written, and traced his signature slowly with one finger, then closed her eyes.

She did not cry. She was past crying. Instead, she was almost happy.

"You found a way out, Dusty," she whispered, remembering the "God bless;" remembering, too, Christmas Midnight Mass in the cathedral.

"You found a way out."

And then suddenly she began to become aware of shouting from the street. It wasn't new, but it had taken a while to permeate her peaceful, quiet surroundings.

Casey opened her eyes, listening for a moment; suddenly a thought struck her, and she leapt up and off the bed, stuffing Dusty's final letter into a hidden pocket somewhere in her clothing and hurrying over to the window.

Seeing a crowd gathered down the road, she slid the window open an inch or so, and put her ear down at the crack, listening.

After about ten seconds of that, she stood bolt upright, staring out at the crowd. It was still some distance away, but her sharp eyes could make out the forms of six or seven gangsters—and two children, one little boy and one teenage girl.

Casey literally flew out of the apartment unit and down the stairs to the front door of the empty apartment building.

There was no door there, but she didn't care as she shot through the moldering door frame, her hands flying automatically to her waist before she realized that she had a belt—but no knives.

She bit her lip, but kept on running, towards the little knot of people in the street.

At first they were oblivious of her approach, but then someone looked up, saw her, and yelled a warning to the others—but too late.

The crowd broke apart as Casey joined them, headbutting one person and tackling another to clear her way.

Before the gangsters could recover, Casey had cleared a path to free the two children, who were indeed Emma and James—Magdalena and Antonio.

They stared as Casey fought, Magdalena surprised and incredulous, Antonio shocked and wondering.

Casey shoved another gangster over—dark-haired Alessandra da Milano— and took a brief moment to smile at the two.

"Run!" she yelled at them, panting as she fought the impossible odds.

Breaking out of her reverie, Magdalena had just enough presence of mind to push Antonio away and tell him to go home.

He stared up at her, with her hands still on his shoulders, his light blue eyes scared and pleading.

"Emma?" he whispered.

"Go," she told him again, firmly.

"Are you going to help Renie?" he asked, regardless.

Finally she nodded, tightening her grip on his shoulders. Her face twisted up for a moment.

"Yeah, I am, Antonio." She ignored the fact that his eyes widened when he realized she'd used his real name. "Just go!"

A moment or so later, Antonio was running obediently down the street without a second glance. Fear leant wings to his speed. However, Magdalena stayed behind, joining Casey in the battle. Minutes after Antonio escaped, the two took off like the wind. Not one of the gang could stop them.

Luigi tried shooting, but by the time he got his gun out and ready they'd disappeared around a corner. Muttering in Italian under his breath, he swore revenge.

Meanwhile, Magdalena and Casey were well on their way to the house. By the time they got back to the house and locked it behind themselves and Antonio, they were out of breath.

Casey promptly sat down against the locked front door, her chest heaving as she gulped for air. Magdalena was in slightly better condition, and she contented herself with sitting down; Antonio did the same.

Casey was the first to look up.

"I'm sorry," was the first thing she said.

"Wha—a—a—at?" Antonio breathed in his confused six-year-old voice. "It's fine!" he assured her, slipping down from his chair and running over to her.

He had absolutely no idea why she would be sorry for anything, but he threw his chubby arms around her in an all-encompassing hug. "Just *stay* with us, Renie!"

Casey stiffened, and then looked up to where Magdalena was still sitting.

The fourteen-year-old Italian girl smiled sadly, a tear slipping down her cheeks as she nodded.

"Stay with us, Casey," she echoed, her voice tight.

Casey shook her head in disbelief. "You can even forgive me after what I've done, Emma?"

The girl nodded simply. "Stay with us. But call me Magdalena."

Thirteen

nd so it was decided that Casey would stay—and that the three
would go by their real names.

As soon as they'd finished their breakfast the next morning,
Magdalena insisted Antonio go outside to play—which he did, in a very bad
temper. He could be seen pressing his face against the window and making
horrible expressions at them, until one or two of his friends came by and he
went to join them in the front yard across the street.

Magdalena kept an eye on her brother through the front window as she
talked with Casey. The older girl finished washing the breakfast dishes, then
sat down nearby.

"Did you get my note?" Casey asked her, and Magdalena nodded.

"Yeah. I wasn't going to go after you, but Ja—Antonio insisted, and I didn't
really want to explain why you were leaving, so I sort of went along with
him."

Magdalena blushed. "I'm not sure it ended all that badly, though."

Casey nodded thoughtfully. "It appears I can't just leave—not yet, at least."

She touched her scar, closing her eyes.

"Once you're here, you're here to stay," Magdalena whispered, more to
herself than to Casey.

The redhead's dark eyes flew open.

"You've heard that?" she demanded.

Magdalena simply bowed her head by way of answer.

"Do you believe it?" Casey pressed.

The fourteen-year-old looked up, straight at Casey. For a moment she hesitated, then shook her head firmly.

"No, I don't. I think you will find a way."

Casey sighed. "Find a way to permanently protect you two, and then go to the police. Yes, that's *very* extremely easy."

"Exactly," Magdalena told her brightly.

Casey laughed shortly. "I don't even know where to begin."

There was silence for a few minutes.

Then suddenly both of them were startled by an unexpected thud on the back door.

Magdalena gasped as Casey tensed, jumping up a moment later.

"I'll go get it," she volunteered in a voice that brooked no contradiction.

Magdalena stood up anyway.

"Wait—" she began, but Casey was already gone.

The redhead approached the back door with caution, waiting silently for about two seconds before flinging it open.

No one was there. Instead, they had left a note—pinned to the door with a knife.

Casey reached out to unpin it and read it—then suddenly she caught movement in the corner of her eye, and froze.

The next moment a second knife came zipping out of nowhere. It was a confident aim, just nicking the side of Casey's neck as it thudded into the door behind her.

Magdalena gasped while, with a grim smile, Casey tore the paper off the door and ducked inside.

"You missed," she called out tranquilly before slamming the door shut, bolting it, and leaning against it.

Magdalena stared at Casey as the older girl casually pressed her hand against the stinging side of her neck and took it away a moment later, wincing.

Her hand came away bloody.

"Got any kind of bandaging?" she asked Magdalena, without taking her eyes off her hand. "And you probably want to call Antonio in."

She glanced down at the torn paper, and stiffened.

"We need to get out of here, *fast*."

* * *

That evening found three travelers—an older, red-haired girl, a younger black-haired one, and the younger girl's look-alike little brother—boarding a train out of Manhattan.

The station and train were crowded. Antonio held tightly to Casey's and Magdalena's hands so that he wouldn't get lost.

In her other hand, Casey held a thick carpet bag—close to her, and tightly. All of them were wearing dark, unobtrusive clothing, and the hood of Casey's jacket was pulled low down over her face.

She kept her gaze on the ground, hoping her scar wouldn't attract any attention—nor the bandage on the side of her neck.

All of the three couldn't wait to get onto the train, where they'd be able to sit down and rest. Casey had made them take the long way, to avoid pursuit.

Now, in the loud, confining press of people, hopefully no one would be able to recognize them.

Finally the train pulled in, and Casey, Antonio, and Magdalena flowed into it along with most of the crowd.

Somehow they managed to stay together, ending up in the same two rows. Antonio and Magdalena sat in one, and Casey sat next to the window in the seat facing them. The seat next to her was quickly taken up by some girl college student who was probably going home for the weekend. After a couple of discreet glances at her, Casey decided she wouldn't be a threat.

Casey assessed the remainder of their surroundings and decided they'd be fine—for the time being. The journey would take hours, though.

Glancing across at Antonio and Magdalena, Casey saw that the two were quickly falling asleep.

She, too, let her head lean forward slightly. But her dark blue eyes didn't close, only narrowing into sleepy-looking but aware slits.

Casey wasn't going to relax until she knew the two children were safe.

And so she watched and waited, during the long hours of their train ride.

One by one, most of the other train's passengers left the train and were replaced. Now Casey had her eyes on a darkly dressed man some rows away from theirs. He had been on the train since Manhattan as well, and now Casey was sure he was watching them—so she returned the favor. But his head was angled away just enough that she couldn't recognize him.

But suddenly, as the train slowed to a stop at the station where Casey had intended getting off, the man turned slightly. His hood fell back, and she caught a glimpse of his face. Only a glimpse.

But Casey knew him right away.

A member of the Manhattan Mafia.

She appeared to relax slightly, leaning back in her seat. Quickly she went over their options in her mind, and soon realized there was really only one.

She couldn't get rid of their pursuer on the train, even if she'd had her knives with her—it would cause too much of a commotion. Besides that, Casey didn't want to be hurting anyone, unless they attacked her—or Magdalena and Antonio.

Their only choice was to get off here after all and try to lose the Mafia member somehow in the city they'd just arrived at—Durham, North Carolina, Casey noted.

Swiftly yet calmly, she shook the two children awake and snatched up their bag, and they got off the train together. Antonio rubbed his eyes annoyedly as he tried to wake himself up. It wasn't quite as cold as it had been in New York, but it was still nighttime.

Casey realized they didn't have time to take detours and such to get rid of the man following them. That would have to wait until tomorrow. After a good night's sleep for all of them.

A *lot* of things would have to wait until tomorrow and the days after. But Casey was confident that, somehow, they'd shake both the gang and the police. Then she would find a safe place for Antonio and Magdalena, and…

And then, she would…

As they walked along, Casey bit her lip. Every survival instinct told her to keep running, even if she was finished being a killer. Not to turn herself in.

But Casey knew now that there was such a thing as justice, and saving her soul—not everything was about survival. She had a purpose in life, and it wasn't just to keep that life.

Casey realized there was only one thing left for her. She was going to have to confess.

She just had to get Antonio and Magdalena to a safe place—first.

Fourteen

"Are you really going to try that, Casey?" Magdalena asked the redhead doubtfully a month later.

The younger girl's black hair was longer now, and she'd turned fifteen in the weeks since they left New York. But her light blue eyes were sadder now, and more thoughtful.

They were sitting on the floor of an old, rundown shed in someone's overgrown field in Florida. A few rays of sunlight shone down from a crack in the roof, and the birds and crickets were making a racket outside, but otherwise all was quiet, except the blowing of the wind around the cracks and crevices of the shed.

Antonio was asleep, wrapped in a blanket and curled up in a corner of the shed. And Magdalena and Casey had just been going over Casey's long-considered plan.

Casey, whose hair was longer now as well, nodded quietly.

"I think it's the only thing that will work at this point, Magdalena. You can take care of Antonio while I'm gone, right?"

"Of course I can!" Magdalena retorted indignantly. "I took care of him for months before you showed up!"

Casey hadn't smiled in a long, long time, but now she did.

"That's true," she admitted. "But you need to be careful. I can't guarantee every single Mafia member will go after me."

"I'll look after him, Casey," Magdalena promised her quickly. "No one will hurt either of us. But… But you'll come back, right?"

The redhead nodded slowly. "If I'm alive, Magdalena, I'll come back. I promise."

"And what are you going to do about that other person who's been following us?" the younger girl wondered.

Casey didn't answer right away. Tracing her scar gently with her finger, she stood up, reaching back and tying her hair back quickly in a ponytail.

She glanced down, and the two girls' eyes met.

"I don't know," Casey said finally. "We'll work that out later. But I'd better go tip off the police," she added, stepping towards the doorway.

She turned as Magdalena jumped up and caught her arm.

"Come back to us, Casey," she whispered pleadingly.

Casey nodded once, then turned to go.

Behind her, Magdalena watched despondently as the older girl left the shed and walked quickly across the field, her profile outlined by the light of the setting sun. Her hair shone red as fire, and eventually she disappeared from view.

Magdalena sat down, clasping something Casey had made for her in her hands. It was a rosary.

As she prayed, Magdalena cried. Even if she had always suspected the truth, it had been wonderful to have someone optimistic and happy like Casey around.

But now Casey was different. She seemed so cold to Magdalena, and even Antonio rarely won a smile from her.

Magdalena reflected bitterly that now they had really lost her. Sure, she was taking care of them, but Magdalena wished Casey had never discovered her identity.

Could it be that Casey's hatred for Nelson Coligny had passed on to Magdalena and Antonio?

Magdalena didn't see the tears that were in Casey's deep blue eyes as the older girl left. Casey did care for the two, very much.

But caring meant that she couldn't let them get too close to her. Sooner or later, Casey knew she was bound to end up either dead or behind bars.

Though if her plan now succeeded, she'd end up with the choice to avoid both. Yet, every moment she spent thinking about it only hardened Casey's conviction that the only thing left for her was to turn herself in.

Alone, she walked the entire distance from the shed to the city, over an hour's walk. By the time she got there, the sun had set, but the darkly-dressed, hooded figure didn't seem to care.

Finding a phone booth, she went inside, pulled paper and pencil out of her pocket, and began to write.

A couple of minutes later she glanced around, emerged from the booth, and after a quick yet cautious scan of her surroundings she set off walking again, more briskly. Towards the police office.

She walked up to a policeman who was just about to head home for the night, and, being careful to conceal her face, handed him the note.

The man was startled, but by the time he'd finished reading the note and gotten even more startled, Casey was gone.

* * *

Walking into the seemingly most popular local pub, Casey didn't bother to glance around too much. She knew that any Manhattan Mafia wouldn't be sitting out in the open, and so it wasn't worth her time to look for them.

Even then, she felt slightly uncomfortable entering the building the way she did, with her hood pulled back and her red hair and scarred face completely visible.

She walked confidently up to the counter, aware that only the most vulgar gangster types would randomly attack a stranger—and that she could definitely handle them with one hand behind her back.

"I'll take a water," she announced loudly and clearly.

The bartender glanced her way.

"Coming right up," he answered absently, struggling with the rapid inflow of customers and perhaps also being irritated that someone would bother him when all they wanted was water. He was busy enough, wasn't he?

Unconcerned, Casey sat down at the bar, idly resting her hands on the counter as she waited.

There weren't many other young women in the pub at the moment, and she definitely attracted attention, even if she was old and tall enough that she didn't seem *completely* out of place.

"Just a water?" someone asked her, and she glanced in their direction, smiling slightly.

"Alcohol can be bad for the nerves," she shrugged professionally, and the man laughed.

"Especially that much," Casey added, eyeing his rather full glass.

"You're not from here, are you," the man observed thoughtfully, raising his eyebrows.

"No," Casey shook her head. "But I'll be back tomorrow."

Even if she didn't seem to notice another of the pub's patrons glance at his watch and leave abruptly, leaving his purchase behind, Casey knew her bit of information had not been unheeded. As she sipped her water slowly, her mouth curved into just a hint of a smile.

* * *

Magdalena was sitting against the wall in the shed, waiting. Antonio sat next to her, blinking but still awake. The girl was tight-lipped and quiet; she wasn't going to cry in front of her little brother, but it wasn't hard for him to see that she was worried about something.

Both of them jumped up when the door began to open. Much to their relief, it was "only" Casey.

"We've been waiting a while," Antonio blurted out immediately as Casey shut the door behind her. "What were you doing?"

"You shouldn't have waited." Casey's eyes were downcast, but then she looked up and smiled. "Did you two have dinner?"

"We did. But you should've come back sooner," Magdalena returned, her voice sharp and irritated. Her light blue eyes were narrowed. "I was worried."

Casey repressed another smile at the younger girl's motherliness, then pulled her hand out of her pocket.

"Well, I brought dessert," she shrugged, and as she revealed a large, red apple, Antonio fairly beamed. "Someone gave this to me. But I don't know if you two are still hungry—"

"I am!" Antonio assured her eagerly, and she passed the apple to him.

He glanced at Magdalena somewhat apprehensively, but she made a sign that he could have the whole thing. Then the girl sat back down, crossing her arms.

"Who gave it to you?" she asked Casey quietly, her eyes still narrow and her voice still angry.

Casey's dark eyes twinkled as she remembered the kindly old woman she'd helped to carry groceries, who'd given her the apple afterwards. "You're a good girl," she'd been told. "There aren't many like you nowadays."

"A kind person," she answered Magdalena softly, and there was something in her voice that forestalled any more questions. As also the remark Casey made immediately afterwards: "Tomorrow will be a busy day. Isn't it time for bed?"

Some minutes later, Antonio was curled up in a blanket, and Magdalena in another, and Casey in a third.

She didn't know that Magdalena was awake for a long time. Casey was uneasy as well.

She was struggling, with herself and with her conscience. Every time she was alone there was nothing else she could think of.

She wanted to live, to be free. It was natural. She was only eighteen, after all.

But she didn't *deserve* to be free. And the thought weighed her down.

Her entire life had been a search for happiness, for a place where she belonged.

And now that she'd found it, was she going to have to let it go—of her own accord?

"Oh God, help me," she murmured to herself over and over again, trying hard not to cry. Trying to believe that everything would be all right.

She didn't want to let her new life go—but she couldn't help but realize that she didn't deserve it.

No one *else* could decide. Her future was in her hands now. Freedom, or imprisonment and possible execution? What was more—ignoring her past, or facing up to it?

She felt that she wouldn't have peace until she decided—correctly.

Tomorrow will be a busy day, she reminded herself. *I should go to sleep. And decide later.*

But no, she realized; she had to decide *now.* And hold to that decision, even if it killed her.

Fifteen

It wasn't hard the next day for Magdalena to see that Casey had reached some kind of conclusion, even if she didn't know what it was. The redhead was strangely more energetic and bright than usual, and today when she wished them good morning the smile was a real one.

She didn't stay at the shed long. After having breakfast with them and warning them to be extra careful, she told them goodbye and set off. They weren't to expect her back until nighttime at least; she wasn't going to return until she was sure she wasn't being followed.

But still, as the day progressed, the siblings got more and more jittery and impatient.

Antonio wanted to play outside, but Magdalena wouldn't let him because Casey had vetoed that. But they both knew that wasn't the real reason behind their irritation with each other.

Magdalena cleaned house with a vengeance, a good deal of her energy fueled from her suspicion that Casey's intention might be to leave the two siblings somewhere and then flee the country.

The very thought disgusted Magdalena—she didn't want to believe it at all. But what else was Casey supposed to do? She couldn't keep the two with her forever, could she? And it would only be a matter of time before the police discovered she was alive.

Leaving the country was the only logical conclusion. Or going back to her original occupation—a possibility Magdalena didn't even want to consider.

Was *everything* a waste of time? Magdalena wondered. Even if she'd suspected Casey's identity from the first, she'd hoped they could change Casey. Because if she turned good, there was no real reason why she couldn't just live a normal life, was there?

But even as she tried to convince herself, Magdalena was forced to acknowledge to herself that if Casey really *did* turn good then she would go to the police and tell them who she was.

It isn't fair, she thought bitterly; but there was no help for it. No matter what Casey chose, Magdalena and Antonio would end up at some orphanage. That was the only viable conclusion.

And so Magdalena swept and scrubbed with a dark, angry energy. Waiting for Casey to return.

* * *

Casey didn't bide long in the pub this time, only popped in briefly, seemed to recognize someone, and left quickly. When the door opened and closed after her, she knew she was being followed.

Glancing at a city clock, she bit her lip and walked even faster; she was going to be late.

She arrived at the predesignated street and glanced around briefly before pulling up her hood. She'd timed it right; there weren't many cars or pedestrians at this time of the late morning.

Casey had vague hopes that the playoff wouldn't be a messy one, but one could never know. Luigi da Milano, hated Casey like poison; and besides that, every one of the Mafia who'd followed Casey to Florida were desperate characters and would take any measures to prevent being arrested.

Casey had only been standing there at the street corner for a few minutes when she heard a once-familiar voice behind her—and that was after she heard the footsteps. "Sicario!"

"Luigi da Milano." Casey took a deep breath before turning around and looking.

It was Luigi all right; with his arms crossed, and his face set in a triumphant smirk, he didn't look too different from how Casey remembered. Neither was the gang behind him any different.

Casey counted eighteen of them. Including the girl a couple of years younger than her, whose face she now remembered: Luigi's daughter, Alessandra.

Even if they had completely outnumbered Casey, the gang still advanced with caution as they surrounded the eighteen-year-old, and Casey couldn't help but smile.

Luigi might have always fancied himself as leader, but his talent was more in brute strength than in tactics. And even if she hadn't tipped off the police, such a crude gathering as this would surely attract any sensible policeman's attention.

Fighting hadn't broken out yet, but already Casey was aware that the city inhabitants around them were suspicious, and some were even hurrying off, probably to fetch the cops. From the looks on the gangsters' faces, a fight was in the air. And from the way they were surrounding the red-haired, scarred teenager, it was only too obvious that their intentions weren't friendly.

"We've got you now, Casey." The gang leader's excitement came through easily in his rough, deep voice.

"Sure as knife," Casey returned sarcastically. "How long ago was it that you 'had' me?"

Luigi took that as an insulting reference to when they'd almost managed to wipe out Casey before, and his face reddened. "We'll finish you off this time!"

"You missed the point," Casey told him softly, standing unflinchingly as her former confederates advanced even closer.

For a moment Luigi was confused. "What?"

"The point of the knife," Casey finished, then bowed her head. "It wasn't even you, was it. You've never killed anyone, da Milano."

"You bet I have, and I'll do it again!" the somewhat thickheaded gang leader shot back.

Casey lifted her head and looked straight at him; at Alessandra who stood silently and smirkingly by his side. "No, you never did your dirty work yourself."

"That's more than you can say," Luigi sneered. "But either way, it doesn't matter to me. Same as you, Casey." His mouth curved into a sarcastic smile.

Casey caught her breath, suddenly remembering that day at the pub in New York, when she'd said she didn't care about killing people.

"I can make that four, sure as knife. I don't care."

But she did care now.

She glanced back at Luigi, suddenly not as cool as she had been. "No, I take that back," she told him fiercely. "It does matter. It does."

Alessandra's eyebrows shot up, and for the first time she spoke.

"You?" she asked Casey incredulously. "It was you who taught me how to kill. What made you change your mind?"

Casey glanced at her in surprise, and for a moment her gaze softened.

"You don't know death until you feel it," she whispered. "You can take lives but you'll never understand until you or someone dear to you loses one."

Alessandra seemed to stiffen, but then Luigi put his hand on her shoulder.

"Enough talk," he snapped, slipping his other hand underneath his dark leather jacket. "Cassandra Sicario. You said a few minutes that I never do my dirty work myself."

"So I did," Casey admitted absently.

The indirect mention of Dusty had brought back memories, and her eyes were brimming with tears. She couldn't deal with these emotions right now, and frantically she tried to push them down.

"Well, this time I will," Luigi remarked, almost offhandedly, as he suddenly retrieved his hand, a handgun in it.

His eyes shone triumphantly as he took careful aim, and the gangsters around Casey backed away.

"You've always been in the way of our success, Casey. I would've killed Nelson and taken his place long ago if it hadn't been for you."

Much to his annoyance, Casey didn't seem to be paying attention. But now she perked up, and a hint of a smile came over her face. Luigi was suspicious, and understandably too.

"What?" he demanded, and Casey shook herself, looking straight back at him. At the gun.

"The police are on the way here," she answered softly, and Luigi actually laughed.

"I don't care," he retorted. "Even if it was true, I wouldn't care. No one is going to save you now. Not some stupid kids, not nobody."

"Knife away," Casey shrugged smilingly. "Or should I say fire away? But you don't even know how to shoot a gun."

Suddenly the gangsters became aware of whirring sirens; not a few of them immediately began to run, and Luigi's face contorted.

"Go, Alessandra!" he told his daughter; then he leveled his gun, directly at Casey, who hadn't moved. "I'm going to kill you for this!"

Casey started walking backwards, slowly at first but then faster. She had no intention of getting shot, nor of getting caught in the police net.

But despite the quickly approaching police forces, Luigi shot once, twice, thrice, and then shouted angrily in Italian as his gun jammed.

Casey felt herself hit in her shoulder, and then in her lower leg.

The third shot missed her completely, but after she walked a few more steps she felt her vision swimming.

She stopped, fighting for breath with her eyes closed.

Suddenly she seemed to see herself in a ditch, with the rain pouring down, and a knife coming down at her—

"You okay?" someone was asking her. Casey's lips moved, but nothing came out. She was so dizzy that she barely noticed when she started falling forward.

She didn't notice when she hit the ground, either. She was unconscious.

Sixteen

Footsteps.

That was what she was hearing. It could only be footsteps—but running ones, not in the same room, but in some hallway.

They were approaching the room, too.

The hospital bed's red-haired occupant opened her dark blue eyes slowly, blinking once or twice before her vision focused on the ceiling.

It was night, she realized; even as she became aware of the bandage on her shoulder, and another on her leg.

Neither really hurt anymore, but suddenly Casey sat up, listening intently to the footsteps.

They stopped just outside the door to her room. And then the knob began to turn.

Even with her perhaps limited childhood experiences, Casey knew enough to know that hospital personnel did not run in the hallways.

Some warning instinct was pressing loudly in her head, and she leapt out of the bed, looking around automatically for some kind of weapon.

There was none.

Though she was injured, her sharp reflexes still worked so well that when the door to the tiny room finally opened, Casey was standing against the wall next to it. She held completely still as the newcomer stepped quickly into the room, walking over to the bed, and gave a quiet gasp upon discovering it was empty.

Meanwhile Casey studied the intruder, recognizing her as soon as the moonlight from the window fell upon her face.

Alessandra da Milano, and a knife with her.

Casey noted ironically that it was one of her own.

She held her breath as Alessandra looked furtively around and then began to creep about the room, looking in every possible hiding place. Casey began slipping out the door while the Mafia member had her back turned.

She would have made it safely out and down the hall without Alessandra knowing a thing, had she not just then tripped over the limp form of the guard just outside the door.

The noise was only slight, but it was enough to alert Alessandra to Casey's location. The younger Italian girl wheeled around, throwing her knife in the same, fluid motion.

Despite her having been trained by Casey herself, the blade thudded into the wooden door, and the next moment Casey was gone.

Hissing in annoyance under her breath, Alessandra darted after her, and a wild chase through the hospital hallway followed; but Alessandra didn't catch up with Casey until they were out of the building.

And even then, she didn't really catch up. She had just a moment to throw another knife at her before Casey disappeared again into the streets' shadows, and she did.

There was a gasp.

She had hit.

Running forward, Alessandra searched some time longer, but her effort only resulted in disappointment. She disappeared herself, muttering angrily.

"You got Dad into jail. I'm gonna find you and kill you!"

* * *

Not ten minutes after Casey and Alessandra had evacuated the hospital, there was another young, feminine figure in the same ground-level hallway they had run through, though this young lady looked significantly different.

Her hair was golden, and her eyes a dark blue-green, and had Casey been there she would have recognized her as the pursuer Casey hadn't been able to identify.

Upon discovering the body of a policeman on the floor in the corridor, the new young woman appeared to be surprised, and her eyes narrowed, but she didn't even bother to go into the room, instead retracing her steps towards the doors to outside.

There she paused, hesitantly biting her lip.

"Let's say I'm Cassandra Sicario," she whispered to herself, taking a deep breath while her sharp eyes roved back and forth. "I woke up in a hospital room, killed the policeman outside, and got out of the building. I'm escaping now. Where do I go?"

After another brief glance around, the girl—who was obviously not Casey— headed for the shadows.

She was tiptoeing tentatively along when suddenly she nearly tripped on something, and it wasn't a cobblestone.

If it hadn't been slippery, it would have cut right through her shoes.

Stooping quickly, the girl picked the object up, and stared at it somewhat confusedly. It was a knife, covered in some dark substance that came away on her hands where she touched it.

The girl didn't have to take it over to a streetlamp to know what that dark substance was.

"Blood, on a knife," she murmured, her eyebrows contracting. "Why? I escape the hospital, and then I knife someone, but I apparently don't kill them…Wait, *how* do I have a knife? The police would have confiscated that."

She mused over that fact for a moment, and then suddenly her eyes widened.

"No, it wasn't me who killed the guard," she realized. "I didn't have a weapon on me. It had to be someone else. And that someone followed me out here…and threw their knife…and missed. But I'm wounded, that's why there's blood on the knife. And the other person…is chasing me, still? Where would I go to escape them? Especially if I was injured?"

The girl listened to the night sounds for a moment.

The hospital was in the outskirts of the city; quite close to the country, really. If she listened hard enough she could hear the wind rustling through the trees, some distance away.

No, not trees; there were no trees around here. Just tall grass.

She closed her eyes, and a picture came into her head. A field, with tall grass. And…a shed. Fallen into disuse…the perfect hiding place.

The girl's eyes opened with a snap, and she glanced between the hospital and the next-door building, peering through the shadows and into the fields beyond. She hesitated, then bent down to replace the knife.

As she did so, she became aware of dark red splotches on the pavement ahead of her. Her path was marked out for her.

She glanced back at the knife, then shook her head and began walking quickly.

"I'm going to regret leaving that behind," she gritted to herself. "But I'd probably regret bringing it, more."

* * *

Antonio was asleep. He'd tried to sit up and wait for Casey to come back, with Magdalena, but the older girl had been taking too long, and he was now enveloped in peaceful slumber, half-wrapped in an old blanket.

Magdalena was still awake, though blinking quite rapidly and obviously in the last minutes before she joined her brother in dreamland.

Suddenly she sat up, pinching herself in an effort to keep herself awake.

She'd heard a sound, and it wasn't just the wind. She'd been hearing that all day; she would know.

This was something else.

Despite her diligent efforts, Magdalena was still blinking when the shed door slowly creaked open.

The girl wheeled around to face it, and breathed a sigh of relief when she saw it was Casey—a sigh of relief that changed into a shriek of alarm when she realized that Casey was about to collapse.

"Casey!" she gasped out as the older, red-headed girl slowly shut the door behind her and then leaned against it, panting.

Casey's shoulder was bandaged, she was limping, and her right arm was bleeding hard. She'd attempted unsuccessfully to wrap it in her jacket, but the blood had soaked through the cloth.

Walking unsteadily into the room, she would've fallen if Magdalena hadn't run forward and tried to support her.

"Casey, what happened?" Magdalena whispered as she tried to help Casey sit against the floor. Antonio was still asleep. "Did you catch the Mafia?"

"Yeah, but they caught me, too," Casey breathed, her breath short. "Magdalena...I think I'm going to faint."

"No, don't," Magdalena protested, her tones sharp from worry. "Don't go to sleep!"

"Can't help it..." Casey murmured dizzily.

She closed her eyes. "Magdalena, you're going to have to wrap it up, okay? I can't. I tried and I can't."

Magdalena stared at the blood-soaked jacket in horror.

"Casey, I don't know how!" She was almost crying now. "I can't do first aid!"

"Put pressure on it." Casey had apparently dealt with somewhat serious injuries before in her assassin career. "And if I pass out, just keep trying to stop it."

"Alright," Magdalena shivered.

Bracing herself, she put her hand over where she judged the blood was coming from, and then jumped back as Casey flinched. "Am I hurting you?"

"No," Casey bit out through clenched teeth. "Take the jacket off—and *keep pressing!*"

Casey's head fell back against the shed wall, and she slumped to a half-sitting position.

Trying to ignore the feeling that she was going to throw up, Magdalena swiftly removed her older friend's dark jacket and tossed it aside.

This time it was easier to see where the wound was, underneath a slit in Casey's shirt sleeve.

Magdalena put pressure on it again, but this time she was frightened when Casey didn't react.

If Magdalena could be more frightened than she already was.

"Casey!" she breathed. "Are you—are you still awake?"

"Yes," came the faint answer; but suddenly Casey's dark blue eyes flew open again. "Shh!"

Magdalena held her breath as Casey listened intently.

Magdalena didn't hear anything, but suddenly Casey's eyes became more alert, and looked straight up, into the younger girl's. "Magdalena, can you hear me?"

"Well, yes," Magdalena returned indignantly.

"Then listen. Wake Antonio up, and get the two of you out of here immediately, do you understand?" Casey's eyes were cold and hard.

Magdalena stared at her, aghast.

"But you're still bleeding!" she protested.

"I know," Casey rasped. "But someone is coming here, and they could very well be a murderer."

"Then they'll kill you," Magdalena retorted. "I'm not going anywhere, Casey!"

"Get Antonio out of here!"

Casey nearly sat up, but Magdalena was holding her down.

"Even if you're going to be stupid, get your little brother out!"

"How much time do we have?" Magdalena demanded, suddenly afraid.

"None," Casey panted, adrenaline screaming through her veins.

But she could see that Magdalena wasn't going to just leave her. "Do you have your jacket?" she demanded. "Yes? Wrap it around my arm, tightly. Yes, like that."

"Is that too tight?" the younger girl asked anxiously, but Casey shook her head.

"No. It's good enough, sure as knife. Now go, Magdalena!"

For what was only half a second but what seemed like an hour, Magdalena hesitated.

Casey realized that the girl needed reassurance. Somehow, Casey summoned enough strength to rise to her feet. She tottered a moment, then leaned against the wall, breathing hard.

"Really, Magdalena—you need to get Antonio out of here, *now*," she insisted, but her voice was even weaker than before.

Reluctantly Magdalena turned to fulfill the command, but it was too late.

Her eyes opened wide in terror as the door swung open, and then even wider in surprise.

The person who stood there, Magdalena had never seen before. But she was sure the person wasn't part of the Mafia.

The girl seemed only a few years older than Magdalena, and she looked completely different as well. Her short, bobbed hair was a bright golden, and her eyes a dark shade of green and blue. Eyes that flamed with anger and resentment when she looked across the tiny room and saw Casey standing there, against the wall.

Maybe the newcomer had been cool and composed before, but now she completely lost it.

"It was you!" she shouted, so loudly that the still-sleeping Antonio jumped up with his eyes wide open. "YOU, Cassandra Sicario! You killed my Dad!"

The girl fairly flew across the room, throwing herself at Casey in a furious gesture. A gesture that was amplified when her fist hit the side of Casey's face with so much force that Casey for a moment saw stars.

She was too weak to offer much resistance as the blows continued, though she knew that even if she could she wouldn't have fought back.

The thought came to her vaguely, even as she slowly slid down against the wall and her eyes fluttered shut, that she deserved this.

She deserved to feel the kind of fear that came before death, the kind of fear she'd given to so many other people.

Except she wasn't afraid, and she didn't think this was death. But everything was so strange and unreal.

Could it be, after all? Yet, all Casey felt was a calmly hopeless peace.

Her vision was fading. But even as she slipped away into unconsciousness, she heard Antonio crying, doubtless startled from his sudden, rude awakening.

Magdalena's screaming was even louder than her little brother's crying.

"Stop. Stop, whoever you are! STOP!"

Magdalena found herself screaming that same word repeatedly, as well as gasping through tears, as she struggled valiantly to pull Casey's attacker off the red-haired girl, who had now slumped completely to the floor.

Finally she seemed to succeed, though both she and the golden-haired girl sat down hard, panting for breath.

Then the stranger began to stand up, and Magdalena grabbed her arm with a desperate violence.

"Stop," she hissed. "You're going to *kill* her!"

The girl looked at her—really looked at her—for the first time, and then fell back limply.

Magdalena's eyes opened wider as she saw the stranger's blue-green eyes flood with sudden, unexpected tears.

"She deserves it," the sixteen-year-old choked out, her voice tight. "She killed my Dad. She killed so many people!"

"She killed mine too," Magdalena told her savagely, but her strong hold on the girl's arm loosened somewhat. "Are you a bad guy?" she asked her cautiously.

The golden-haired girl's face looked blank. "No? I'm Trisha Lee. My dad was a detective. But he was good. He didn't deserve to die!"

"A detective?" Magdalena asked softly, and Trisha nodded. "But then you should know that it's wrong to kill people."

Magdalena's brain was racing. How could she protect Casey?

To her surprise, Trisha's face softened, and then she covered her face in her hands. But Magdalena could see the older girl's shoulders heaving as she wept.

"But… It's not fair. She stabbed him in the back. He didn't have a chance. She deserves to…" Trisha's voice trailed off inaudibly.

Magdalena bit her lip, but she could tell that this Trisha person, whoever she was, was completely, emotionally frustrated.

But suddenly Trisha looked up at her. "She murdered your dad, too? And you…"

Magdalena glanced briefly at her brother, whose fright was gradually subsiding.

"We've forgiven her," she told Trisha finally, in a low voice. "We gave her a chance—"

"A person like her *deserves* no chance!" Trisha shouted, her fists clenching. "I ought to… I…"

"Take deep breaths," Magdalena advised. "That's what she always tells us. Take deep breaths when you're angry."

Trisha stared at her in disbelief. "You…"

Her voice broke off as she drew a deep, shuddering breath, and the two girls sat together silently for a few minutes.

After a few minutes of silence, Magdalena glanced at Trisha questioningly. Her heart sank as she saw that the older girl's face was still hard-set and angry, though a trifle surprised.

"Did I just knock her out?"

"She was already hurt." The words sounded even harsher than Magdalena intended them to be, and she half-winced. "She just got a gang of Mafia arrested, and got stabbed, and I don't know what else."

"Shot, twice," Trisha supplied quietly, and it was Magdalena's turn to look surprised. "They took her to the hospital. I was going to visit her there but it seems someone else was there before me. Probably the same one who stabbed her."

Magdalena was horrified when Trisha suddenly smiled. "I guess I'm not that bad of a detective after all."

The puzzle was starting to come together for the younger girl.

"You're the one who's been following us," she realized, and Trisha nodded. "The one we weren't able to shake off."

"I guess that *would* be me," Trisha admitted; but then her eyes narrowed. "Did you take care of her wound?"

"I don't know," Magdalena told her, and suddenly all her fears came out in a rush. "It was bleeding so bad. It probably still is. I don't know how to take care of it. I don't know how to do *anything!*"

Trisha stood up. She walked over to Casey's limp figure, then bent down to inspect the older girl's arm. "Hmm. Let's see..."

* * *

The first thing Casey was aware of was the pain. Dull, but irritating. Her arm ached. And her shoulder. And her leg. And she was so tired.

But she could hear people talking, though what they said she couldn't tell. Eventually she managed to open her eyes, though they were overwhelmingly heavy.

Her vision faltered for a moment and then focused on the roof of the shed.

"...Awake now, I guess." The gibberish she was hearing began to take form into words. "Cassandra? Cassandra Sicario?"

The thought came to Casey that no one but enemies called her by her full name, and she winced involuntarily.

But someone was helping her sit up. No, two people. Magdalena and Antonio.

Casey could see them now, but she could also see the golden-haired stranger, and her eyes narrowed, tired as she was.

"You're from Manhattan," she identified, and the girl nodded, flushing slightly.

Casey couldn't help but notice that she looked both flustered and annoyed.

"I am," Trisha told her coolly. "I'm with the police there, as well."

"Aren't you a little young for that?" Casey asked frankly.

Trisha's cheeks grew redder, but she didn't answer the question directly. "My name is Patricia—Trisha—Lee. Ring a bell?"

"Not really," Casey had to admit, after a moment's thought.

Trisha's face twisted. "Of course not," she supplied sarcastically. "You've murdered so many people, you don't even condescend to remember their names!"

Casey glanced at the shocked-looking Antonio, and then at Trisha again.

"Talk about this somewhere else?" she demanded. "You don't need to—"

"Yes, I do!" Trisha interrupted her, her eyes flashing. "I'm going to get you arrested. And them, too!"

Suddenly Casey sat up straight, looking directly at Trisha.

"No, you aren't," she returned sharply. "I don't know who you are, but it doesn't matter. These children are innocent, and you're going to help me find them an orphanage!"

Antonio burst into tears, and Magdalena looked stricken. But none of it affected Trisha in the least.

"That comes second," she shook her head. "Even if you've made these kids think you're reformed, you aren't going to fool me. You won't be getting away again!"

"No, you don't understand," Casey put in. "I'm not getting away. I… Never mind, you wouldn't understand," she realized, biting her lip. "Fine. But you have to help me with the kids. And then I'll turn myself in."

It was Trisha's turn to stare, and Magdalena's and Antonio's as well. But Casey kept speaking before any of them could.

"I suppose it was selfish of me to keep them with me so long," she sighed, dropping her weary gaze to the floor. "I should have left them somewhere in Manhattan. I was just afraid…"

"You were afraid the Mafia would find out about us," Magdalena realized, and Casey nodded.

"But now they're all in prison, except for that one that got away and tried to kill you," Trisha finished. "Do you know him?"

"Him?" Casey managed a small smile. "It's a her. But that's none of your business. I'll be telling that to the police if they ask me."

Trisha fairly spluttered in indignation. "But you—"

"No, I'm really going to go to the police station, and you can come with me if you insist."

Casey's gaze lowered even farther.

"I just want to make sure Antonio and Magdalena will be safe first. It's my fault they're in this situation in the first place."

"No, it isn't, Casey!" Magdalena broke in, her eyes tearing up. "We're here because we wanted to stay with you. We want to stay with you forever!"

Casey looked up, at the two of them, and her voice was startlingly calm.

"I have my own path to walk, Magdalena. Where I go, neither of you must ever follow. You're going to lead your own, normal, innocent lives—do you understand me?"

"But Casey…" Magdalena's voice was tearful, and Antonio's face horrified.

"Casey, you can't go anywhere!" he shouted at her; then he literally hurled himself forward, flailing with his small, pudgy fists. "You're not going anywhere without us! You aren't…you can't…"

Finally he stopped and fell quiet, as Casey wrapped her arms around him tiredly. But she smiled.

"So you see, Miss Lee. I have to protect them. And that also involves finding the last Manhattan Mafia member here in Florida and getting her to where she can't do any harm. But to be honest, I think I'll need your help for that."

Angry as she was, Trisha wasn't going to let an appeal like that go by.

"Of course I'll help you," she told Casey indignantly. "I'm going to be a detective once I'm older—and once you're where you belong!"

"I'm gonna be a lawyer," Antonio put in suddenly from Casey's lap. "I won't let them have my Casey!"

"How old is that kid?" Trisha muttered in disbelief.

"I'm six!" Antonio told her, with an air of pride.

"Well, good for you," the golden-haired girl shrugged.

She looked at Casey again, and her eyes narrowed.

"Fine. I'll help you find that Mafia person and get these kids somewhere safe. But don't you realize they'd have been safe if you just took 'em to the police in the first place?"

"And don't *you* realize that if anyone has no confidence in the abilities of the police force, it's me?" Casey returned quietly. "I can't even count how many times I've gotten past their 'protection'."

Trisha shrugged again. "Suit yourself," she said finally. There was silence.

But then Magdalena spoke up. "Casey, they aren't going to... We'll be able to see you again, right?"

Casey lifted her hands in a typically Italian gesture of ignorance. "I don't know, Magdalena, okay? But whatever happens, I want you to remember something... I want you to carry a message for me."

Magdalena leaned forward. "What is it?"

"A lot of teenagers nowadays seem to think that gangs are cool—you know that, right?" Casey continued as Magdalena nodded wordlessly.

"Well, as you've been able to see for yourself... Gangs aren't cool at all.

"Trying to be bad, or even just thinking of it as 'cool,' will ruin your life forever, sure as knife, in one way or another. Too many people are headed the wrong path, and I hate to think what'll happen to them. I know you are convinced, Magdalena, but will you carry this message for me?"

Casey's dark blue eyes were filled with a deep, yet hopeful kind of sadness.

"I'll probably never be free again... But I want to make sure the world knows. Or a small part of it, anyway. You're young and innocent; you can let the sunlight shine on so many other lives..."

Magdalena covered her face in her hands. She was crying.

"I'll tell them, Casey!"

<h1 style="text-align:center">Epilogue</h1>

It was only about a week later that a darkly dressed, hooded, tall red-haired girl of about eighteen or nineteen walked up the steps to the police station in Manhattan, New York.

She paused in front of the door. She was looking at it, but from the reflection in her eyes it was obvious she was seeing something else.

Or remembering.

Her eyes were a hauntingly sad dark blue, and there was a large scar on her left cheek, not to mention the bandages that were visible on her arm and shoulder.

She looked like she'd been in an epic fight. But from the calmly peaceful expression on her face, she looked like she'd won that fight as well.

Casey took a deep breath before putting her hand on the knob and turning it. She hesitated a brief moment before actually pushing it open and stepping inside.

"Who's that?" someone at a desk asked, without even bothering to look up.

Casey leaned against the door, breathing hard. She pushed her hood back.

"Cassandra, sure as knife. Cassandra Sicario."

Finis.

About the Author

Gabrielle Marie Kozak is an American author whose fiction explores pressure, endurance, and the cost of refusing to surrender oneself to oppressive systems. Her debut, *The Trooper Series*, began as a body of work written before she graduated high school and introduced her recurring focus on individual sovereignty under strain.

The eldest of nine children, Gabrielle spent nearly two years as a religious sister before turning her attention fully to writing and publishing. Her stories center on those who carry responsibility, those who break beneath it, and those who survive when systems fail.

She lives in Nebraska and loves writing, coffee, and all things Poland.

Website: **gmariaek.com**

Also by Gabrielle Marie Kozak

Thank you for reading!

If this story stayed with you, I would be grateful if you'd consider leaving a short review. Reviews help books like this find the readers who need them.

Your time, your attention, and your support truly matter.

If you'd like to continue reading my work, **The Trooper Series** is the best place to start.

Trooper A1: The Purple Blitzkrieg is the first book in the series.

Trooper A1: The Purple Blitzkrieg
SHE LOST HER BROTHER - JUST NOT THE WAY SHE THOUGHT.

Moira Whyte refuses to believe the **bloody evidence** that confirms her brother's death. Instead, she begins to hack into **Encephalon**, the underground network built to **subjugate the entire world.**

She's right. Her brother isn't dead.

He's worse than dead.

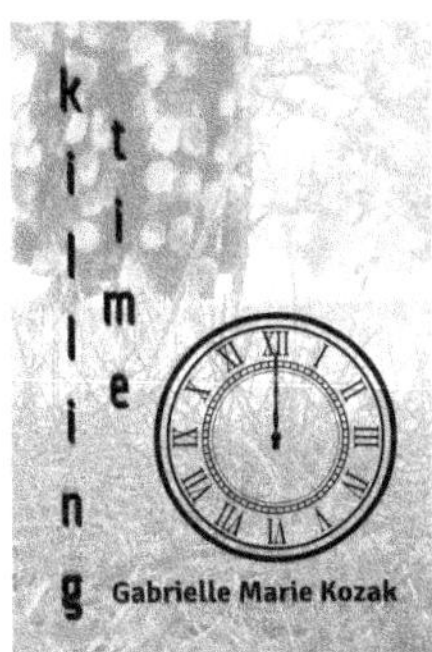

Killing Time

SHE'S ACCUSED OF BEING A SERIAL KILLER - WHILE THE REAL ONE IS HUNTING HER.

Pietro Dola thought his career was normal—until he walked into a hospital room with a team of police and saved the life of an orphaned teenager he was supposed to arrest.

Now he's asking the impossible question:

how can Elvira Thyme be a serial killer...

when the real serial killer is hunting Elvira?